I0640588

Alfred Paget

Shakespeare's plays : a chapter of stage history

An essay on the Shakesperian drama

Alfred Paget

Shakespeare's plays : a chapter of stage history
An essay on the Shakesperian drama

ISBN/EAN: 9783337305345

Printed in Europe, USA, Canada, Australia, Japan

Cover: Foto ©Andreas Hilbeck / pixelio.de

More available books at **www.hansebooks.com**

SHAKESPEARE'S PLAYS:

A

CHAPTER OF STAGE HISTORY.

AN ESSAY ON THE SHAKESPERIAN DRAMA.

By A. H. PAGET.

LONDON:
JOHN WILSON, 12, KING WILLIAM STREET, STRAND.
1875.

Price One Shilling.

PREFACE.

THE following pages were originally prepared as a paper to be read before the Leicester Literary and Philosophical Society, early in the present year; and, at the time of its delivery, I had no intention of their appearing in print. Since then, however, suggestions kindly made by Mr. J. O. Halliwell, Mr. C. Roach Smith, and other gentlemen qualified to advise, have led me to venture upon publication; and I now lay my essay, in a slightly enlarged form, before such of the general public as take interest in tracing the connection of Shakespeare's works with the English stage.

A. H. P.

April, 1875.

SHAKESPEARE'S PLAYS:

A CHAPTER OF STAGE HISTORY.

THE title of this paper, I trust, fairly indicates
the subject proposed. It does not treat of Shakespeare personally; nor of his plays, described simply
with reference to himself. There is no attempt to
show how the plays became what they are; I simply
take them as they stand, and try to show what has
been done with them since they came from the mind
of the poet. I want to tell something of the conditions under which they have been presented during
a long series of years; for although Shakespeare is
so much more to us than a mere writer of stage
plays, I dare assert that now, as in his own day, the
theatre is his proper and most natural home. He
may be studied and dearly prized in all places; but to
know Shakespeare in his fulness, without the agency
of the stage, is, to my mind, as impossible as to
taste the magical charm of snowy peaks and glaciers
only from poring over books of science at home.

Our concern, then, is less with the great Original
than with those men through whom, for better or

worse, he has been made known; the dramatists who have handled his plays, and the actors who have been the living embodiments of his creations. It is a wide field of research, and a lecture can only point out a few of its features. The temptation to pile up great names, and say a little about everything, must be resisted. And, so, looking to the real drift of the matter, and trying to find for this paper the most exact description, I have ventured to call it 'A Chapter of Stage History.'

It would seem best to begin with an account of the Elizabethan theatres, in order to explain how Shakespeare's plays were first acted, and that we might call to mind under what outer conditions he wrote as he did. But this of itself is ample subject for a lecture, and, awaiting further instalments from Mr. Halliwell of his 'Illustrations of the Life of Shakespeare,' the task would be somewhat hazardous. The company of players to which the poet belonged travelled about, performing in noblemen's mansions, inn-yards, and civic halls; in our own Townhall, Mr. Kelly has told us.* But they were chiefly engaged at two theatres in London, the Blackfriars, and a large circular or polygonal playhouse, the Globe, on the Bankside. The buildings were simple in form; in the larger theatres only the stage, the 'tiring rooms, and galleries were roofed over, the central space, or yard, being open to the sky. There must have been plenty of shouting and

---

* 'Notices illustrative of the Drama and other Amusements at Leicester,' by William Kelly.

bluster on the stage, and rough manners among the audience. There was no scenery; the walls were draped with tapestry or curtains, and other curtains placed between the front of the stage and the back, called traverses, increased or lessened the visible area, according as they were drawn together or thrown apart. There was then nothing of the stage illusion that forms so large a part of modern theatrical displays. The actors were left on a naked platform, to tell the poet's story by their own unaided efforts.

Now, we may well believe that there were real advantages in this simplicity and freedom from the restraints that the attempt to produce scenery would have imposed. There was then nothing to distract the mind: old tapestry and traverses suggest no comparison with the outer world of real life. *We* are not always so fortunate: for ill-painted landscapes and bad architecture do. And more than that; when he desired, Shakespeare drew in his own words the background of his plays. Had less been asked of the imagination of others, Shakespeare would have given fewer hints to guide their fancy, and much exquisite description of nature might never have been penned. In writing the History of King Henry the Fifth, he seems to have keenly felt this inability to do more than suggest, and he boldly challenges the good-will of his audience assembled at the Globe. Perhaps nowhere, in the whole range of the drama, could be found so powerful an appeal of the kind, as the noble speech at the

opening of this play. The poet calls upon his
hearers to take their part in the illusion; for without
their lively sympathy he can do nothing for them.

" O for a muse of fire, that would ascend
   The brighest heaven of invention !
   A kingdom for a stage, princes to act,
   And monarchs to behold the swelling scene !
   Then should the warlike Harry, like himself,
   Assume the port of Mars; and, at his heels,
   Leash'd in like hounds, should famine, sword, and fire
   Crouch for employment. But, pardon, gentles all,
   The flat, unraisèd spirit that hath dared
   On this unworthy scaffold to bring forth
   So great an object : can this cockpit hold
   The vasty fields of France ? or may we cram
   Within this wooden O the very casques
   That did affright the air at Agincourt ?
   O, pardon ! since a crooked figure may
   Attest, in little place, a million ;
   And let us, ciphers to this great accompt,
   On your imaginary forces work.
   Suppose, within the girdle of these walls
   Are now confined two mighty monarchies,
   Whose high upreared and abutting fronts
   The perilous, narrow ocean parts asunder.
   Piece out our imperfections with your thoughts,
   Into a thousand parts divide one man,
   And make imaginary puissance.
   Think, when we talk of horses, that you see them
   Printing their proud hoofs i' the receiving earth :
   For 'tis your thoughts that now must deck our kings,
   Carry them here and there, jumping o'er times,
   Turning the accomplishment of many years
   Into an hour-glass ; for the which supply,
   Admit me, Chorus to this history ;
   Who, prologue-like, your humble patience pray,
   Gently to hear, kindly to judge, our play."

On what, then, did Shakespeare rely, for the

working out of his conceptions? On good acting, and that only. The age that produced great dramatists produced great actors also; the two were cast in the same mould, and, in several cases, the same individual was at once actor and dramatist. The mighty lines of the poet called forth the actor's genius; and the poet himself, hearing his words sent back to him with the added force of impassioned utterance, wrote in confidence that his thoughts would be understood and realized. This held good with every portion of a play; for we read that leading actors did not then disdain to undertake small parts besides their chief character. And thus servants and messengers were presented by men of the highest stamp; a thing not often seen on the modern stage.

It is a common regret that it is so hard to judge of actors of a former age. We wish to know how actors whom we are used to see, would compare with the great men of past days. We can read descriptions of their playing, collect scraps of anecdote that prove their genius, study their portraits; but we come away, after all, very little satisfied, and with a mighty hunger for more exact information. The further back we go, the greater this uncertainty becomes: in the infancy of an art the standards of comparison are indefinite, and the data for exact analysis are wanting.

This applies in a high degree to our knowledge of the original acting of Shakespeare's plays. We have, indeed, the names of the chief performers of the day; but we cannot do with them, as we might with the painters of former times, set side by side works by Raphael and Rembrandt, or of Holbein and Gainsborough, and nicely weigh the manner of each master. We cannot thus set the art of Burbage by that of Betterton, nor feel on sure ground in balancing the merits of Garrick's tragedy and Kean's.

But there is no doubt whatever that the greatest actor of Shakespeare's day was Richard Burbage. He played Shylock, Richard III., Prince Henry, Romeo, Henry V., Brutus, Hamlet, Othello, Lear, Macbeth, Pericles, and Coriolanus. Probably, in every case too, Burbage was the original performer of these parts; and it is amazing to think of the good fortune of an actor to whom it fell, to be the creator on the stage of such a wondrous round of characters.

Burbage lived long before the days of professional critics; and except from mention of his name in legal documents relating to various theatres, and from a few poems, we know but little about him. The list of his characters is taken from a manuscript epitaph in the British Museum, which, though not a brilliant poem, has a few expressions that convey real ideas.

> "Tyrant Macbeth, with unwasht, bloody hand,
> We vainly now may *hope to understand.*"

Without Burbage, the written character would be an insoluble riddle.

"Thy stature small, but every thought and mood
　Might throughly *from thy face* be understood ;
And his whole action he could change with ease,
From ancient Lear to youthful Pericles."

Truly Burbage had taught this man something
worth knowing. Here is clear insight into the whole
art of acting; a piece of sound dramatic criticism
from one who had thought the matter out for himself, and had received his impressions direct. This
was probably written soon after Burbage died, in
1619. Another poem, dated 1672, by Richard
Flecknoe, tells that, he " ne'er went off the stage
but with applause;" and, with a finer artistic discernment, that he was "beauty to the eye, and
music to the ear." But we must accept this eulogium
with caution. Fifty years had passed since Burbage
died, and the lines must have been the embodiment
of tradition rather than, as in the last case, the
outcome of the writer's own vivid recollection.

Bishop Corbett in his "Iter Boreale," written
about 1620, gives trifling, but genuine, evidence of
the place this actor filled in the popular mind. He
tells that when an innkeeper at Bosworth was describing the fight there, he let slip the name
of Burbage for that of King Richard.

" And when he should have said, King Richard died,
　And called—a horse ! a horse !—he, Burbage, cried."

Touching and very brief is another well-known
epitaph—exit Burbage.

But Comedy bears equal rank with Tragedy in

Shakespeare's plays. A race of professional jesters had long existed ; and at this time the stage took to itself these free wits, and their talents became public property, instead of, as till then, the sole possession of persons of rank. Tarleton died somewhat early in Shakespeare's career ; but his successor, William Kempe, was the favourite low comedian of his day. He was the original Dogberry, and probably played Launce, Launcelot Gobbo, the Gravedigger, Touchstone, and Justice Shallow. Shakespeare wrote his low-comedy parts more fully than had been usual before that time, and as he meant them to be played. He hated gag :—" Let those that play your clowns speak no more than is set down for them."

One broad distinction divides this period from our own. There were then no women on the stage, and women's parts were filled by boys or young men. This usage, I fancy, has had its bearing upon the plays themselves. In the induction to The Taming of the Shrew, a page is dressed to personate the wife of the supposed lord, and the whole thing seems perfectly natural. Coriolanus is said to have gained an oaken chaplet, when " he might act the woman in the scene ;" that is, " ere his youth attained a beard." The performer of Rosalind, in 'As you like it,' after allowing that it is "not the fashion to see the lady the epilogue," goes on with the words, " *if I were a woman.*" Hamlet thus greets one of the players who come to Elsinore : " What ! my young lady and mistress ! By'r lady,

your ladyship is nearer to heaven than when I saw
you last, by the altitude of a chopine. Pray God,
your voice, like a piece of uncurrent gold, be not
cracked within the ring." Surely, this is not the
language of the prince to a woman, but to a growing boy, whom he was used to see *as a woman*.
Now, it would seem that Shakespeare turned this
condition of his own times to a real, dramatic purpose. How many of his heroines put on man's
attire! Imogen wanders in Wales as a boy; Julia
follows her faithless swain, and becomes his page;
Viola, in the guise of Cesario, attracts the love of
the Countess Olivia; Rosalind carries on a mock
courtship with her lover in the forest; Portia con-
ducts a case before the Doge of Venice. Shakespeare knew that his boys were best *as boys*, and so
let his fancy run in this channel. The old custom
of actors of repute taking apprentices to study under
them, provided boys for these parts. Nathaniel
Field was one of the most famous of these "woman-
actors;" he was a contemporary of Shakespeare's,
and may have played some of his heroines. At a
later date, Kynaston was noted in the same line:
both were fine tragedians in after life.*

The history of any subject will naturally divide
itself into sections, or groups of facts, according as

---

* In 1629 some French actresses appeared at several London
theatres in succession, but met with small encouragement. We may
hear more of women on the stage at an early date, but there is
abundant evidence that the commonly accepted view as to their
absence is, in the main, correct.

certain agencies come into play, are expended, and give place to new. The foregoing depicts one portion of our dramatic history, more clearly defined, indeed, than any later period. When the Civil Wars broke out the theatres were suppressed, and, with the restoration of Charles the Second, begins a fresh chapter of the history of the English stage.

The circumstances that produced the altered aspect of this second dramatic epoch, and gave its distinctive tone, were in part social, and in part purely literary. In the days of Elizabeth the nation was instinct with patriotism and love of liberty. Those were the days of high hopes and mighty aspirations. Upon the vigorous stock of mediævalism was engrafted the restless spirit of enterprise and inquiry; and the result to letters was a sudden meridian of poetry. But the day of romance was soon gone : the best intellect of the land had been absorbed in a fierce domestic struggle, and the issue of twenty years of strife was such as to bring feelings of doubt and shame to honest men of all parties. And thus the keen spirit of the last age had given place to a prosaic temperament, little apt to produce a noble race of poets.

While, in our country, literature had been brought almost to a stand by the Civil Wars, its development had been rapid in France. The French nature has more love for finish and exactness of form in writing than the English, and an eagerness for rules that shall fence off exuberant growth from the pale of perfect refinement and propriety. In

1636 was founded the French Academy, and in 1659, Corneille, having elaborated certain ideas, faintly suggested by Aristotle, and, to some extent, carried out in the practice of the Greek dramatists, published his famous essay on the Unities of the Drama; of time, namely, of place, and of action. Here, then, was established a new code of dramatic laws, and a memorable instance given of a man's ingenuity misapplied.

Charles, and the immediate friends, who afterwards formed his Court, and who set the fashion in literary taste, from their residence abroad, were acquainted with these new rules of writing; and French modes soon prevailed in this country.

The primary concern of the stage of any period is, of course, the plays written for it by its own authors; they deal most with the interests of the day, and reflect the passing tone of thought and feeling. We have hitherto seen Shakespeare as a contemporary writer, the master-mind of the existing school. But the few years of the suppression had snapped the thread of continuity, till then the sole tradition of the stage. A fresh era had been ushered in, and Shakespeare and his brother poets were now the men of a bygone age, who were set in competition with the new writers of the day.

But these elder poets still held their ground, and it is noteworthy that Beaumont and Fletcher's plays were more acted than Shakespeare's; and it seems to have been a debated point whether Shakespeare or Fletcher was the greater dramatist. Langbaine, in

2

his account of the English dramatic poets,* enume-
rates twenty-three plays by Beaumont and Fletcher,
from a total of fifty-two, as having been acted since
the re-opening of the theatres; whereas only about
fifteen of Shakespeare's are distinctly mentioned in
a similar list. The four grandest tragedies— Macbeth, Hamlet, Lear, and Othello—were then, we
learn, stock plays; the classic pieces were Julius
Cæsar, Antony and Cleopatra, Timon, Troilus and
Cressida, and Coriolanus. From the English Histories were played Richard II., Henry IV., and
Henry VIII., and among the more purely imaginative
poems were Cymbeline and The Tempest. But the
statement that these plays were acted is only partially true; they were acted, but with a difference.

For we now enter upon a novel phase of our subject. According to the new French rules, the grand
poetic freedom of Shakespeare, his power of moving
about in time and space in defiance of the unities,
was licentious irregularity. He was, indeed, a striking writer, but he lived in a barbarous age, and sadly
wanted form. His plays, therefore, were taken in
hand by men who corrected their faults, and improved them for those more critical and enlightened
times. Incidents and characters were struck out,

* "An Account of the English Dramatick Poets. Or some Obser-
vations and Remarks on the Lives and Writings, of all those that
have publish'd either Comedies, Tragedies, Tragi-Comedies, Pastorals,
Masques, Interludes, Farces, or Opera's in the English Tongue. By
Gerard Langbaine. Oxford. Printed by L. L. for George West and
Henry Clements. An. Dom. 1691." A scarce volume in the possession of the writer.

and new were inserted ; the language was reformed ; music and show were introduced ; and thus Shakespeare's plays, as presented on the boards, took the impress of the shallow and vicious tastes of that day.

For example, what was *called* The Tempest, or *The Enchanted Island*, was a piece arranged by Dryden and Davenant, with music by Henry Purcell. The Cymbeline was by Durfey, and was styled the *Injured Princess, or The Fatal Wager*, and, no doubt, the change was more than skin-deep. Richard II. was rechristened the *Sicilian Usurper*, and Coriolanus *The Ingratitude of a Commonwealth*, both being the work of Nahum Tate, one of the compilers of the New Version of the Psalms. In King Lear, also, Tate adopted a singularly bold treatment of the text, introducing love-passages between Edgar and Cordelia, giving the old King victory over his foes, and a happy ending to the piece. Timon was an alteration by Shadwell, afterwards poet-laureate. Troilus and Cressida, or *Truth found out too late*, was again by Dryden, and he, too, turned Antony and Cleopatra into *All for Love, or The World well lost*. Sir William Davenant, laureate to Charles I. and Charles II., combined materials from Measure for Measure and Much Ado into his *Law against Lovers :* but Davenant's masterpiece was Macbeth.

If all these productions had been merely ephemeral little importance would attach to them, and they would hardly be mentioned here. But this is not the case. In some instances these and similar adaptations held the stage for years and years, nay, still hold it ; and one of my chief objects is to show that what for generations was played and accepted as Shakespeare was not Shakespeare, but some dilution of him prepared within the last two centuries. Davenant's Macbeth is a case in point. This tragedy, as we see it performed, contains a great deal more than we can find in our books, and we wonder where the supernumerary witches come from, and what is the meaning of " Locke's celebrated music," paraded in the bills. We notice that whereas Shakespeare employs his witches most sparingly, just so far as needed to pitch the key of the drama, and no more, in the acted play the stage swarms with witches, and witches of another species from the three weird and ghastly beings for whom Shakespeare has imagined a new dialect and a new nature scarce half human. But the intellectual standpoint of Shakespeare was above Davenant and those for whom he catered. The Italian custom of blending music with action had been naturalized in France, and came over here with other French fashions. Accordingly he turned Macbeth into a sort of melodrama, with interpolated songs and choruses set by Matthew Locke. After seventy years, indeed, Davenant's version was laid aside ; but scarcely a manager has yet ventured to present Macbeth without these clumsy musical scenes, which cling like brambles to the skirts of the tragedy, delay its progress, and are utterly foreign to the true spirit of the poem.

Samuel Pepys, an inveterate play-goer, saw Mac-

beth more than once acted in this form, and no doubt
his words express the general opinion of his day
upon the merits of the piece. We must remember
that Pepys was no critic, and never troubled himself
as to whether dramas were original or adapted, and
probably knew very little of Shakespeare from books.

He enters as follows in his Diary under the date
of January 6th, 1666-7 :—"To the Duke's house,
and saw 'Macbeth,' which, though I saw it lately,
yet appears a most excellent play in all respects, but
especially in divertissement, though it be a deep
tragedy; which is a strange perfection in a tragedy,
it being most proper here, and suitable." In
November of the same year he witnessed another
of these adaptations. It was The Tempest, "an
old play of Shakespeare's." He says it was "the
most innocent play" that he ever saw, and describes
a curious trick in the music for managing an echo.
He considers that "the play has no great wit, but
yet (is) good above ordinary plays."

Some of Pepys's theatrical notes are too amusing
to be passed over, while considering the debased state
of the Shakesperian drama in his day. On March
1st, 1662, he saw Romeo and Juliet "the first time
it was ever acted, but it is a play of itself the worst
that ever I heard." The next year he went to see
King Henry VIII. at the Duke's theatre. He calls
it "made up of patches, nothing but show." "The
Merry Wives," he says, "did not please me at all
in no part of it." The Taming of the Shrew, in
spite of "some very good pieces in it," he considered

" but a mean play." It is clear that Pepys did not much care for Shakespeare, at least as his dramas were then presented. For one play his contempt was without measure. He writes for September 29th, 1662, " To the King's Theatre, where we saw ' Midsummer Night's Dream,' which I had never seen before, nor shall ever again, for it is the most insipid, ridiculous play that ever I saw in my life."

The number of theatres in London was far less at this time than formerly. It is not easy to give an exact list of the houses open at any one date, but there must have been a dozen or fifteen in existence in the reign of James I. A few are lost sight of before the suppression ; and on the re-establishment of the stage two grand companies were licensed by the King, one styled His Majesty's Servants, and the other taking their title from the Duke of York, afterwards James II. The King's Servants were soon settled in Drury Lane under a patent granted to Thomas Killigrew. The Duke's Company had several removals, sometimes acting in theatres in or about Lincoln's Inn Fields, and sometimes in Dorset Gardens, below Fleet Street, and were under the direction of Sir William Davenant. The lists of standard plays to be acted by these two companies were fixed by the Court and their own alternate choice; the dramas of Shakespeare, Fletcher, and Jonson were divided between them, and neither was suffered to invade the repertory of the other. In 1684, owing to the decay of some of the elder actors, it was found mutually advantageous to unite the companies, and for ten years the King's House was the one theatre open, with Betterton as the leading tragedian.

Among actors, Thomas Betterton is the central figure of this era, as Burbage was of the last. He began his career just before the Restoration, and continued on the stage till his death, in 1710. He was the greatest actor of the day in Shakespeare's tragedies, and we know him by the descriptions of Pepys, Steele, Aston, and best of all, as judged by a fellow player, Colley Cibber. Pepys enters the following in his Dairy for August 24, 1661:

"To the Opera (that is, Davenant's Theatre,) and there saw 'Hamlet, Prince of Denmark,' done with scenes, very well, but, above all, Betterton did the Prince's part beyond imagination." Seven years later, after seeing the same play, he writes that he was "mightily pleased with it, but, above all, with Betterton, the best part, I believe, that ever man acted."

Steele saw him buried in Westminster Cloisters, and, with a full heart, writes of his excellencies, and tells in what high estimation a nation should hold such an artist.*

These are sincere and valuable testimonies to the greatness of Betterton: but Cibber's practical knowledge of the art of acting gives special value to his evidence.

"Betterton was an actor," he writes, "as Shake-

---

* 'Tatler,' May 4th, 1710.

spear was an author, both without competitors!
formed for the mutual assistance and illustration
of each other's genius!" * * *

"Could how Betterton spoke be as easily known
as what he spoke, then might you see the Muse of
Shakespear in her triumph, with all her beauties
in their best array, rising into real life, and charming her beholders. But, alas! since all this is so far
out of the reach of description, how shall I show
you Betterton? Should I therefore tell you that
all the Othellos, Hamlets, Hotspurs, Mackbeths, and
Brutus's whom you may have seen since his time,
have fallen far short of him; this still should give
you no idea of his particular excellence. Let us
see, then, what a particular comparison may do,
whether that may yet draw him nearer to you."

He then describes his Hamlet, in the first scene
with the Ghost. He began, he says, " with a pause
of mute amazement; then, rising slowly to a solemn
trembling voice, he made the Ghost equally terrible
to the spectator as to himself." Betterton had a
fine sense of individuality in the portrayal of character. The wild starts and flashing fire of Hotspur were distinct from the occasional irritation of
Brutus. To the alternation of rage and tenderness
in Othello he gave a force and beauty long remembered. His style seems to have combined the
boundless freedom and variety of nature, with the
highest dignity of an ideal school of acting; the
latter an element inherited by immediate followers,
while the former essential was almost lost sight of,

until revived by Garrick. In person he had little
natural grace : for his figure was thick-set and rather
clumsy, nor had his voice much sweetness or beauty
of tone. But, in spite of all defects, Betterton's
aspect was majestic and venerable, and when he entered the scene the eyes of all were fixed upon him.

Of his sound understanding and correct ear,
Cibber writes,—"I never heard a line from Betterton
in tragedy, wherein my judgment, my ear, and my
imagination were not fully satisfied." He heard this
great actor say " that he never thought any kind
of (applause) equal to an attentive silence : that
there were many ways of deceiving an audience
into a loud one, but to keep them husht and quiet
was an applause that only truth and merit could
arrive at." These words show the true artist :
would that others had power to hold their hearers
like Betterton, and wisdom to know where their
strength should lie !

Colley Cibber, here mentioned as a critic, was an
important man in his day ; he was actor, play-writer,
manager, adapter of Shakespeare, and afterwards
poet-laureate. Cibber's version of Richard III. is
still the Richard of the stage ; and from the mere
fact of its vitality, apart from its obvious merits, his
play demands notice almost above any similar production. The purport of this adaptation is to con-
centrate attention on Richard, by still further black-
ening his portrait, and by withdrawing lateral interests : by striking off the wings of the story. Cibber
produced a work excellently fitted for the stage,

but at the loss of much that is grand in the original.
Cibber's is an effective, but a coarse, play.

As Shakespeare wrote it, this is one of a series of
historical dramas: closely connected with it are the
three plays bearing the name of King Henry VI., in
the last of which the future King Richard bears an
important part. Now, as these were not then acting
plays, Cibber took from them some fine speeches, in
which Richard's character is carefully drawn, and
the scene in which he murders the King in the
Tower. That is utilization of waste material, and
pardonable where the principle of wide deviation
from an acknowledged work of art is once allowed.
So, also, the total omission of the Duke of Clarence,
with his famous dream, is well judged. For stage
effect his part is not only over-weighted, considering
the small figure he makes in this portion of the
story, but, by its elaboration, is actually detrimental
to a more important scene in the drama.

But the inherent vulgarity of the play, as revised,
is shown by an interpolated passage, in which Richard
deliberately sets himself to kill his wife by neglect
and cruelty. Equally commonplace and morbid is a
scene in which we are brought to the very threshold
of the chamber where the children are smothered,
and there see Richard prowling about and moralizing
on his wickedness. The language of the piece is a
compound of Shakespeare and Cibber, curiously
interlaced; for, besides the omissions and interpolations, he habitually debases the poetry to his own
standard of dulness. Impassioned ejaculations of

grief and horror seemed profane when the stage had become a mere amusement, and were set aside. The glorious blank verse of the Elizabethan writers was then out of date; its rhythm was not understood. The accented *ed*, for instance, in the verb and participle jarred on Cibber's sensitive ear, and he would always change a line to avoid it. Thus, when Norfolk gives the King the paper, found in his tent :—

> "Jockey of Norfolk, be not too bold,
> For Dickon thy master is bought and sold,"

Richard boldly declares it—

> "A thing devisèd by the enemy."

That would not do for Cibber; he wrote—

> "A weak invention of the enemy."

Again, recurring words in a line were inartistic. After that awful night on Bosworth Field, with the shades of his victims : (and here Cibber has been at the pains to re-write the vision, and has cut out the agony of remorse and the frenzied self-examination at its close :) when aroused to arms, Richard exclaims—

> "O Ratcliff! I have dreamed a fearful dream."

Cibber has it :—

> "O Catesby, I have had such horrid dreams."

Notice, too, that the crack rants in the part of Richard are Cibber's own invention.

Such are—

> " Off with his head! So much for Buckingham."

A tremendous hit on the stage. So again—

> " Richmond, I say, come forth and singly face me,
> Richard is hoarse with daring thee to arms."

And, lastly—

> " Hence babbling dreams, you threaten here in vain;
> Conscience, avaunt! Richard's himself again."

Perhaps these time-honoured points tell as much in favour of Cibber's version as its general practicability.

Immediately after the Restoration, women began to appear on the English stage, and it is pleasant to remember that Mrs. Betterton was the best actress in Shakespeare's plays. We have Cibber's word for this, and Pepys also sounds her praise. Mrs. Betterton first appeared as " Ianthe," in a play by Davenant, and Pepys habitually calls her by this name. One day he saw the Duchess of Malfi " well performed, but Betterton and Ianthe to admiration." Another time it was the Bondman, and he writes, " Betterton and my poor Ianthe outdo all the world."

After Betterton came Barton Booth, a man of the highest culture, and of the most imposing dignity and grace of manner; but who was apt to become dull, being without the highest inspiration of his master.

Booth is remembered as the Cato of Addison's tragedy, and his best Shakesperian part was Othello. His contemporary Wilks was a fine Shakesperian actor, and played Hamlet well. By nature he must have been a light comedian ; his was an easier, more natural style than Booth's ; but in tragedy at times he wanted repose and weight. Cibber, the partner of these two men in the management of Drury Lane, in spite of grave defects of voice and person, acted a few of Shakespere's tragic parts ; giving them, no doubt, strongly marked individuality, or, as we might say, playing them as " character " rather than as tragedy. He acted his own Richard, Iago, and also Cardinal Wolsey. This last is interesting. Till that time the leading part in Henry VIII. had been the King himself. In Shakespeare's day the stage treatment of Henry was a delicate matter ; it would not do to assign this part to an inferior actor, and set the King at a disadvantage beside the Cardinal. Hence arose a tradition : Booth played King Henry, and thus it was that an actor who allowed himself to be scarcely fit for tragedy, ventured to enact a character out of which Kemble afterwards made a striking stage-figure, if not an accurately historical portrait.

It is here convenient to pass over a few years, and come at once to the time when Shakespeare's plays, after a dull epoch, again held the foremost place on the stage. In 1741, David Garrick, an unknown man, played Richard III. at an out-of-the-way theatre in London, and at once sprang into fame. In 1747 he became joint patentee of Drury Lane, and set about the renovation of the Shakesperian drama. Now begins, though in an uncertain, tentative fashion, the restoration of the genuine text of the plays. Garrick announced Macbeth to be performed " as written by Shakespeare." What could this mean ? The age was uncritical, and had long accepted a spurious Shakespeare in perfect good faith. The great actor, Quin, knew no more than the public. He was startled at the vigorous, uncouth words of the original, and asked Garrick where on earth he had got such strange language. Locke's music, I believe, he retained; no doubt, it lightens the play, and helps to make it go. But Garrick relied on his acting ; he carefully taught Mrs. Pritchard, his best actress, and by them the parts of Macbeth and the Lady were created anew. Garrick got together a grand company of players, and trained them in the study of Shakespeare; and during nearly thirty years of management he placed a considerable number of Shakespeare's plays upon his stage. But in speaking of Garrick as a reformer, and he was one in many ways, we must remember the general taste of his day. The bearing of modern poetical thought is towards ideality ; it strives to reach above and below the visible, and to deal with subtleties and the inner significance of things. But this depth and refine-ment of fancy lay beyond the concerns of the shrewd, bustling manager, eager to draw the town by an effective representation. Garrick cast aside base traditions, but he fashioned new.

That the plays should be acted literally " as written by Shakespeare " was then, as it now is, out of the question ; but as one who took unwarrantable liberties with the plots, characters and language, Garrick, like Falstaff, might count himself " little better than one of the wicked." Probably every play he brought out was disfigured, more or less, by interpolations and injurious omissions. But his adaptation of Hamlet is a curiosity of bad taste, and he candidly confessed that his producing this play with altera- tions, was " the most impudent thing he ever did." In Hamlet the story advances steadily to a certain point ; but, in the latter scenes, the action is slow. The King is so very delicate in suggesting that Laertes should assassinate his nephew ; Hamlet has so much to explain to Horatio about what has hap- pened since they parted, and Osric is so very profuse, that we are a long time in getting over the ground. And in the fifth act of a tragedy it is a bold thing to bring on fresh characters to make us laugh while waiting for the funeral of a gentle girl. Hamlet's death is not glorious, it is simply very sad ; and the close of the play is singularly melancholy, and, in a way, untheatrical. To write a showy drama was the last thing in Shakespeare's mind ; events fall out in Hamlet just as they might in real life. But a play that is without ostentatious poetic justice is apt to seem tame and unsatisfactory to minds trained to look for it at every turn. Garrick felt these diffi- culties with growing force ; and at last he declared that he would not leave the stage till he had

" rescued this noble play from the rubbish of the
fifth act." Very near the end of his career, he
prepared a stage version without the gravediggers ;
he made the King, when attacked, defend himself
manfully, and brought down the curtain with plenty
of bustle and effect. This arrangement of the plot
served the remainder of Garrick's time ; but, soon
after his death, was happily laid by and forgotten.

Many years before, Garrick had produced Romeo
and Juliet, re-written by himself, and, sad to say,
his version still holds the stage. It is the same
story over again as Cibber's Richard, and every old
adaptation of Shakespeare ; all must be plain, and
lie on the surface. The poem, as it stands, was
complicated, he thought, wanting in clearness and
point. What business had Romeo with a previous
suit ? The answer is that in this lies half the
meaning and beauty of the story. In Romeo,
Shakespeare shows an unreal, sentimental affection
shrivelled up to nothing before the fire of true love.
But Garrick failed to see this ; at one stroke his
early passion is swept away, and Juliet's name is
brought prematurely forward, to hold the place of
that of the scornful Rosaline. Again, in the last act :
how weak, he thought, for the lovers to die, and not
exchange a word, when so much might be made of
the scene ! And so, by a happy thought, he lets
Juliet wake in her tomb, before the poison which
Romeo has drunk has taken effect, and there was a
fine situation ! He carries her in his arms down to
the footlights, and the two talk pure Garrick verse,

till the potion does its work, and Romeo expires in
torture before the eyes of Juliet. All this is excellent good sense, and has been much admired as a
capital sermon preached by Shakespeare. But what
has become of the poem? Whenever this play,
still called Shakespeare's tragedy, is acted, we have
before us, not the "pair of star-crossed lovers,"
the enthronement of ideal devotion and purity amid
bitter surroundings, but a dismal warning against
imprudent attachments and the follies of youth.

But we cannot understand what Garrick did for
Shakespeare, unless we know what he was as an
actor. When he appeared, Quin was the foremost
man on the stage; he was a sterling comedian, but
in his hands tragedy had moved far away from
nature, and was little more than stiff, conventional
declamation. We read of Quin's pomposity, his
"sawing" and "grinding" delivery, his "pumping"
and "paving" gestures. Tragedy was then spoken
in a monotonous chanting tone, without pause or
variety. Garrick was of a quick and fervid nature,
and this made his acting what it was. He broke up
the measured declamation by startling pauses and
striking gestures; he was all spirit and life; his
voice was animated, his figure graceful, and his
brilliant eyes darted fire in all directions. Quin and
his colleagues of the formal, solemn school felt their
empire vanish like smoke before the daring in-
novator. "If this young fellow is right," he said,
"then we have all been wrong." Pedants alleged
that Garrick played in defiance of the rules of

grammar; that he paused when he ought to go on,
and went on when he ought to pause: that his
acting was affectation—mere clap-trap. But the
world knew better, and the public verdict followed
the summing-up of the author of the Rosciad :

> " When in the features all the soul's portray'd,
> And passions, such as Garrick's, are display'd,
> To me they seem from quickest feelings caught;
> Each start is nature, and each pause is thought."

Garrick's most formidable rival was Barry, the
finest stage lover of the day. He was tall, which
Garrick was not, and had a voice of the utmost tenderness and beauty. One season the town was thrown
into excitement by these two tragedians playing
Romeo against each other; and though superiority
in specific scenes was claimed for each, we may well
believe that Barry's rare personal gifts gave him the
advantage. But when, some years later, Garrick
and Barry were acting Lear at the same time, the
public voice was less divided. We may picture
Garrick as the graceful, dashing hero of high
comedy, and the clever actor of eccentric character;
but we can clearly see that beyond and above all
this were heights of poetic inspiration, and the
simple pathos of nature.

> " The town has found out different ways
> To praise the different Lears ;
> To Barry they give loud huzzas ;
> To Garrick only tears."

And again,

" A king, nay, every inch a king,
Such as Barry doth appear;
But Garrick's quite a different thing.
He's every inch King Lear."

Before leaving this part of the subject, it would
be unfair to pass over the name of Charles Macklin.
He is chiefly remembered now as the writer of The
Man of the World; but, in his day, he did good
Shakesperian work, and, in respect of two plays,
the Merchant of Venice and Macbeth, he deserves
to rank high as a reformer. In their early days,
Macklin and Garrick were close friends : they dearly
loved their profession, and were bent on breaking
down the false style of acting then in vogue. And
in this, Macklin got the start. A few months
before Garrick came to the front, he acted Shylock
in a new fashion. At that time the received play
was a modification of Shakespeare's, by Lord Lans-
downe, and the Jew was a ludicrous character played
by low comedians. Macklin changed all that: he went
to the true text, and gave to Shylock his proper
dignity and passion and pathos. When quite an old
man, Macklin made an equally startling innovation
in playing Macbeth in kilt and tartan. Garrick
never ventured on this ; he feared the ridicule of the
public ; for they were used to see stage personages
either dressed as ordinary ladies and gentlemen, or
in wonderful garments, meant to be correct, but
revealing a strong undercurrent of the attire of that
day. No doubt, Macklin's Macbeth was a very
incomplete portrait, and would seem now, as, for

reasons directly opposite, it seemed a century ago,
little better than a snuff-shop Scotchman. But as
a bold onward step towards the reproduction of
historical costume for stage purposes, Macklin's
experiment should be gratefully recorded.

I have dealt rather largely, and severely too, with
the debased stage versions of Shakespeare's plays ;
and it might naturally be supposed that I would
have the plays acted precisely after the stage directions given in the ordinary text. But it is time to
take up the other side, and show this to be an im-
possibility. There are such things in dramatic
workmanship as neatness of construction and skill
in developing a plot. It is easier to put down several
short scenes, as many as may be wanted, each dealing
with a single group of characters, than so to marshal
events that a few comprehensive scenes shall advance
the story in various departments with smoothness
and regard to probability. But how different the
pleasure of an audience in the two cases ! Consider
the fulness and harmony and *sense of delusion* in
such a scene as the fourth of the second act of King
Henry IV., Part I. In a single picture we have
Prince Henry's jest with Francis, Falstaff's account
of the adventure on Gadshill, which is truly marvellous every way ; and after all that is done, we get
the acted interview between the king and his son,
and wind up with the visitation of the sheriff, and
the searching of Falstaff's pockets as he lies asleep
behind the arras. A grander comic scene was never
imagined ; and our being enabled to see so much of

the characters at one view gives an air of reality to
the whole that cannot be overrated.

As a contrast to this, compare the last act of
Macbeth. How broken up and fidgetty it is! What
harassing recollections we have of pieces of painted
woods and fortifications clapping together and sliding
apart; of little stage armies marching across, with
drums and trumpets sounding from behind; of a few
words being spoken, and then—a fresh scene! A
room in the castle at Dunsinane, the country near
Dunsinane, another room in the castle, the open
country again, a place within the castle, a plain
before it, and another part of the same plain, pass
before the eye during this one act. Now, I am not
a stage-manager, and do not propose how this is to
be remedied; but I do say that no one would dare
to write in this fashion now. The writer would so
arrange his materials as to carry on the story without these rapid and wearisome changes of scene,
which require a constant agility of mind to follow
their movements, and never let us forget that we
are in a theatre.

Of course we must take into account the altered
condition of the stage in a period of three centuries.
In Shakespeare's day, as before stated, the appoint-
ments of the London playhouses were very simple.
In King Henry VIII. some unusual pageantry is indicated by the stage directions. The Queen's trial
at Blackfriars, the coronation procession of Anne
Boleyn, the vision of the spirits and the christening
of the Princess Elizabeth, were clearly meant as

gorgeous spectacles. The stage must have been
crowded with splendid figures, attired and arranged
with the greatest care ; but there is no correspond-
ing description of scenery ; and the records of that
time show that only the rudest attempts were made
to realize the localities of the various parts of the
plays.

In this, at all events, we have improved since the
sixteenth century ; and it stands to reason that the
noblest works should be presented with all possible
aids to comprehension and enjoyment, that they
may not be at a disadvantage compared with pieces
written for the stage as it now is. In producing
Shakespeare's plays, therefore, regard must be had
to the effective management of the scenery. It is
always an evil to shift the scenes before the eyes
of the spectators, that is, during the progress of an
act ; consequently, other things being equal, the
fewer the (dramatic) scenes are in number in excess
of the number of acts, the smoother and more
delightful will be the performance. And more than
that ; the fewer (painted) scenes there are to pro-
vide, the more care and expense can be bestowed on
each. And thus we have ample motives for striking
out superfluous matter, for occasionally altering the
sequence of incidents *as told*, and even for joining
together different passages in the same play, where
the fusion tends to true dramatic effect. Of course,
manipulation of this sort may be done well or ill :
to do it well requires both tact and poetic feeling,
as well as strict reverence for the meaning of the

writer. But treatment such as this is very different
from the method of the old adapters; they retained
just so much of the original as suited their purpose,
and then seasoned what was left, according to taste,
with whatever they chose to consider wanting to
make their dish complete.

Again, the change in social manners since the days
of Elizabeth and James the First furnishes another
reason for departing from literal exactness. We do
not now, either in real life or in our literature,
tolerate the grossness of ideas and language that
is so common with the old dramatists. This freedom of speech is matter of historic interest to
avowed students; but the mass of those who go
to see plays are neither students nor philosophers,
but simply an abstract of the world at large. A
heavy responsibility rests with those who, except
for grave and unanswerable reasons, suggest base
thoughts to audiences composed of men and women
of all ages, ranks and degrees of culture, or ac-
custom them to associate debasing sights and coarse
words with the pleasures of the theatre. I am
aware that this trenches upon the whole question
of the action of the stage upon public morals,—a
topic I have no wish to handle. But, writing as a
regular play-goer, one who has faith in the stage,
and would willingly do it a service, I fairly say that
I sometimes wonder at what seems to me a professional blindness to impropriety. It is, no doubt,
the result of tradition, and a survival of former
times. But we must look to it; for this is the bar

that shuts out from our theatres many who should
be there to lend their influence in raising an institu-
tion that has in it the elements of the highest good,
and that no amount of censure can ever destroy ;
but which must be a blessing, or a public curse, in
proportion as it finds its chief support among persons
of character or the dregs of society.

But, to return to purely artistic questions. Many
of the plays are too long to be acted as they stand,
if judged by our modern ways of life ; and it is easy
to find passages, just a few lines here and there, or
even whole scenes, that may well be excused upon
the stage. Till lately, audiences in London lived
within a comparatively short distance of the
theatres. Now it is far otherwise. Many persons
travel a long way to reach their homes ; some must
catch the last omnibuses or local trains, or the
night trains into the country. This makes them
impatient of anything like prosiness, for they are
afraid of not getting away in time. It is sad to see
half the spectators rising to their feet and moving
off, while the players are still speaking on the stage;
but managers learn to accept this discourtesy, and
cut short the endings of plays as far as can be done.
And, after all, taste in certain matters will differ
from one age to another. We fancy we have a
nicer sense of the value of time than our fathers,
and in everything study condensation and brevity.
In imaginative writing a line of thought may be
worked out or simply be indicated. Much modern
poetry aims at suggestion rather than elaboration ;

many things are left to inference, which we must
trace for ourselves. Judged from our present standpoint, Shakespeare is apt to be wordy in closing his
tragedies. Take Romeo and Juliet: the lovers are
dead; the tale is told, and we know what we ought
to think about it. How wearisome would all that
follows be, if played to the end! The watch enter
the churchyard, and are active in the discharge of
their duties; the prince and the heads of the rival
houses are summoned, and grieve for what has
happened; and Friar Laurence, while disclaiming all
desire to be tedious, recapitulates most of the action
of the story. We should not be interested to see
Montague and Capulet shake hands, nor care much
for the quaint tag set down for the prince.

> " For never was a story of more woe
> Than this of Juliet and her Romeo."

There is undoubted pleasure in feeling that something is withheld from our eyes and ears, which the
poet entrusts to our inner sense; and I more than
half believe that this formal closing of an account
is best omitted. The effect of the last scene in
Hamlet would be less striking were the curtain not
lowered as the prince dies in the arms of Horatio.
Or in Othello, if anything were said after the Moor,
first throwing off their guard, with the cunning of a
suicide, those standing by, has stabbed himself and
fallen dead. So, too, in Macbeth, if instead of the
death of the tyrant upon the stage, and the final rush

and cheer of the soldiers; his head were brought in
stuck on a pole, and the play ended with a speech
from the new King, in which he promises promo-
tion to all his friends, and invites them to see him
crowned at Scone.   It is, I believe, most impressive
and dramatic to bring down the curtain close upon
the catastrophe, and, at all risk, to avoid an anti-
climax.   Nothing tends to destroy effect like hanging fire at the last.   Modern writers know this well,
and, in the words of Benvolio,

> " The date is out of such prolixity."

It is not my plan to give more than a brief outline
of the course of the Shakesperian drama onwards
to our own day.   Much has been written upon the
great players since Garrick ; and what they did may
easily be learned from books.   When Garrick died,
Henderson was the first Shakesperian actor ; he
was short-lived, but in spite of great personal dis-
advantages, made his mark both in tragedy and
comedy.   Then came Mrs. Siddons, whose celebrity
has almost blinded us to the fame of Mrs. Cibber,
Mrs. Pritchard, and the tragedy-queens of the last
century.   With the Kembles, with John Philip
Kemble especially, a more studied elocution came
into vogue ; perhaps in the grandeur of his person
and the dignity of his style, this actor more resembled
Barton Booth than any one else before or since his
time.   Then, once more, came the reaction.   Cooke
appeared, who was the Shylock, Iago, and Richard
of his day.   It has been said that he represented

"the slang and bravura of tragedy," and he declared that he would "make Black Jack (*i. e.* Kemble) tremble in his shoes." The daring nature of Cooke's acting reached a still higher development in the hands of the elder Kean, who professed a great admiration for Cooke. Kean had many points of resemblance to Garrick. Both were small and elastic in figure, were rapid and graceful in motion, had marvellously piercing eyes, and took their time with the words of a part in defiance of established rules. They were both men of quick and nervous temperament, and both destroyed and created schools of acting. Kean had not great versatility; he did little in comedy, was not a writer, nor even a manager, and never influenced public opinion except through one channel. But as a tragedian we are tempted to believe that he surpassed Garrick; that is, where bursts of overwhelming fury and deadly hate could avail. His Macbeth and Hamlet and Romeo were good only in parts; his Richard III. must have equalled Garrick's, and his Othello was grander beyond all comparison, for Garrick could make nothing of the character. Edmund Kean's is not a happy name in dramatic records; the story of his life is very melancholy. But, viewing him simply as a tragic artist, we can only wonder at his mighty genius.

Kemble's management was marked by the increased attention given to the Roman plays. Such characters as Brutus and Coriolanus specially suited his distinguished appearance and manner; and as the plays were then getting to be acted with rather more correctness of costume and scenery than before, these pictures of classical life became very popular. Kean seems to have troubled himself little about the text of the plays, and generally acted them as they came to hand. An adaptation of Richard II., after the old fashion, was written for him, but it soon fell into disuse. One reform we do owe to Kean : he restored the proper ending to King Lear. Macready was a wise and energetic manager, as well as a powerful actor, and worked hard and successfully to make the public appreciate Shakespeare. Under him the plays were produced in greater purity of form, and with a higher degree of artistic completeness, than ever before. We may expect to learn much of interest from the ' Reminiscences of Macready,' as edited by Sir Frederick Pollock.

Since Macready's time there have been two notable managements in London in which Shakespeare's plays have been the chief feature ;—that of Charles Kean at the Princess's Theatre, and that of Mr. Phelps, at Sadler's Wells. At the Princess's a long series of plays were ably presented, all put on with the strictest regard to correctness of scenery, costumes, and accessories. Mr. Kean was an excellent antiquary, and spared no pains nor expense to make these " revivals" perfect lessons in archæology. He assumed the position of a public teacher more than any other manager.

Mr. Phelps's course was singularly honourable.

He took a small outlying theatre, then at the very lowest ebb of disrepute. He first set himself to establish decorum in his house, and then, gradually gaining power over the humble audiences of Clerkenwell and Islington, he trained a public to enjoy and understand the poetical drama when truthfully and intelligently set before them. Mr. Phelps enlarged the Shakesperian repertory to an extent altogether beyond precedent; and has himself, probably, played more of Shakespeare's characters, and succeeded in parts of more widely different types, than any actor on record. One example of his tact must suffice. No drama has been more tampered with and distorted in various attempts to fit it for the stage than 'A Midsummer Night's Dream.' What Pepys thought of it when acted has been already shown, and, till lately, no one imagined that it could be performed as written. In dealing with this play, Mr. Phelps, as usual with him, stuck to the original text, and made of it a delightful entertainment, while maintaining throughout the spirit of the poem. And more than that: it has been left to Mr. Phelps to show that the character of Bottom the Weaver is a really fine part for an actor.

A few years ago, Mr. Fechter, then lessee of the Lyceum Theatre, drew considerable attention to the tragedies of Hamlet and Othello, from some novelties in the mode of presentation. His position as a London manager puts him on a different footing from that of several eminent foreign players, who have, from time to time, acted Shakespeare in this

country, and whose names are omitted from this
sketch. Since then, Mr. Calvert has conducted a
series of Shaksperian performances at the Prince's
Theatre, Manchester. His method most nearly re-
sembles that of Charles Kean ; and, like him, Mr.
Calvert sometimes interpolates scenes, purely for
the sake of scenic effect. In this particular, I think
the judgment of both has been at fault ; but difference of opinion as to matters of detail must not
blind us to the good work done.

Lastly, we must look forwards, as well as back on
the past. During several years an actor has been
preparing himself for the highest walks of his profession ; and training us, at the same time, to follow
an artist who can display for us the depths of a
man's heart. History repeats itself : the interest
excited by Mr. Irving is such as that awakened when
Garrick, and afterwards Kean, brought new life and
fresh individualities to bear on an old theme. After
a single attempt in the drama of Shakespeare, we
cannot pretend to tell what career may lie before
Mr. Irving, nor say to what renown he may attain.
But if any should desire to settle his place now in
the roll of players, I would turn to the old regret
that it is so hard to compare actors of past and
present times. How can we set in the same scale
the evidence of our own senses and those of other
people ? To persons who are simply aghast at Mr.
Irving's yells and the glare of his eye, I would say
that they little know this artist. Let them watch
him from his first entry upon the scene till his

departure, and note the grace, the subtlety, the breadth and the repose; the shifting lines of thought mirrored in that wondrous face; the wealth of attitude and gesture, that form an endless series of pictures and suggestions of infinite delight; and their powers of appreciation and sympathy for art will grow by what they feed on. If to rush along on the whirlwind of passion, like Kean, to fascinate by marvellous strokes of nature, like Garrick, to appal by the horrors of a stricken conscience, like no one but himself, and to be, like Burbage, "beauty to the eye, and music to the ear;"—if to succeed in all this is to be a great actor, then, most assuredly, such an one is Irving.

But it will be said that I am romancing, and deluding myself with words. I trust not; but my field of vision is limited, and what we see and hear for ourselves goes for more than description at second-hand. I write only as I feel; that Mr. Irving is one who may show us the glories of the Shakesperian drama, so dear to our forefathers, even in a degraded state. And I further believe that, through men such as he, and by the faithful setting forth of Shakespeare's designs, adorned by every worthy means at our command, we may gradually attain to a fuller knowledge and a deeper understanding of the soul of poetry.

PRINTED BY J. E. ADLARD, BARTHOLOMEW CLOSE.

MR. SWINBURNE'S

"FLAT BURGLARY"

ON

SHAKSPERE.

TWO LETTERS FROM

THE "SPECTATOR" OF SEPTEMBER 6th & 13th, 1879.

BY

F. J. FURNIVALL.

LONDON:

TRÜBNER AND CO., LUDGATE HILL.

———

1879.

[TO THE EDITOR OF THE "SPECTATOR."—SEPTEMBER 6TH.]

SIR,—Mr. Swinburne is always so grateful to have his mistakes about Shakspere corrected, that I am sure he will thank the *Spectator* for allowing me to assure him that he need not take away from Shakspere the credit of having written *The Tempest, King John, Richard III., Venus and Adonis,* and *Lucrece,* as he has lately done, by certain assertions of his in his amusing comment on *Edward III.*

1. On the word "rarieties," in that play, Mr. Swinburne writes, "Another word indiscoverable in any genuine play of Shakespeare." But the folk whom Mr. Swinburne calls "sham Shakespeareans" know the word extremely well in the first Folio of their Shakspere's Works, in whose first play, *The Tempest,* on p. 6, col. 2, "rariety" occurs twice within three consecutive lines :—

Gon.—But the rariety of it is, which is indeed almost beyond credit.
Seb.—As many voucht rarieties are."

2. On the word "endamagement," in *Edward III.,* Mr. Swinburne notes, "Yet another non-Shakespearean word; this time a Gallicism" (!). Yet the "sham Shakespeareans" know it as an old friend in their Shakspere's *King John,* first Folio, "Histories," p. 5, col. 1 :—

" These flagges of France that are aduanced heere
Before the eye and prospect of your Towne,
Haue hither march'd to your endamagement."

3. On the *Edward III.* "invocate," Mr. Swinburne writes, "A pre-Shakespearean word, and proper to the academic school of playwrights." Yet "sham Shakespeareans" know the word well, in their poet's "Sonnets" and *Richard III.:*—

" Be thou the tenth Muse, ten times more in worth
Then those old Nine which rimers inuocate."—*Son.* xxxviii., l. 10.

"Thou bloodlesse Remnant of that Royall Blood,
Be it lawfull that I inuocate thy Ghost,
To heare the Lamentations of poore Anne."—*Rich. III.,* I., ii. 8.

4. On the *Edward III.* "wistly," Mr. Swinburne says:—" This word occurs but once in Shakespeare,—*Richard II.,* Act. V., sc. 4." The "sham Shakespeareans," however, know it two or three times more. In stanza 58 of *Venus and Adonis,* l. 343,—

" O what a sight it was, wistly to view
How she came stealing to the wayward boy ! "

" She thought he blush'd as knowing Tarquin's lust,
And, blushing with him, wistly on him gaz'd."—*Lucrece,* l. 1,355.

" The sun look'd on the world with glorious eye,
Yet not so wistly as this queen on him."—*Passionate Pilgrim,* vi. 82.

May we not, then, define Mr. Swinburne's " sham Shakespearean " as one who knows his Shakspere, and a " Swinburnian Shakespearean " as one who does not ?

Surely, of all shams in matters Shaksperean, the greatest is that of a man pretending to be a judge of Shakspere's words and style, sneering at others for not knowing them, and yet declaring shamelessly that words used by the poet in *The Tempest, King John, Richard III.,* the *Sonnets, Venus and Adonis,* and *Lucrece,* are not his. When will Mr. Swinburne learn modesty ?—I am, Sir, &c.,

3 *St. George's Square, N.W.*   F. J. FURNIVALL.

[TO THE EDITOR OF THE "SPECTATOR."—SEPTEMBER 13TH.]

SIR,—I did not last week state the full extent of the "flat burglary" that Mr. Swinburne has committed on Shakspere. There are three more plays of which he has tried to rob our dramatist, namely, the *First Part of Henry IV., Cymbeline,* and *Coriolanus.*

Our newswoman here lets magazines for a penny a read. Thinking Mr. Swinburne's article might be worth that honest coin, I paid it, read the performance, noted its main mistakes, and saw there were others. Out of that pennyworth I wrote my first letter. But as Mr. Swinburne's article was really not worth twopence, I asked his publishers to give me a copy of it for nothing, which they kindly did. Then I found that Mr. Swinburne had "conveyed" the *First Part of King Henry IV., Coriolanus,* and *Cymbeline* from Shakspere, as well as the *Tempest, King John, Richard III., Venus and Adonis,* and *Lucrece.* This is what Mr. Swinburne calls genuine Shakspere criticism, as opposed to the "sham" stuff that he, in such choice billingsgate, denounces. If he will but write another like article or two, he will come to the result that Shakspere never wrote any plays or poems at all; and then, of course, we who believe he wrote a great many must be shams indeed, in what Mr. Swinburne is pleased to call his mind, or his judgment. But to the proof of this further burglary of Mr. Swinburne's. In answer to Edward III.'s demand for her love, the Countess of Salisbury opposes this proposal, that he should kill her husband and his wife; and the King then says,—"Thy *opposition* is beyond our law." And on this use of "opposition," Mr. Swinburne comments :—"Yet another and a singular misuse of a word never so used or misused by Shakespeare" (p. 342, note). But the word is used in just this sense, of "that which is set against, by way of combat or comparison," in the *First Part of King Henry IV.,* II., iii., 15, First Folio, *Hist.,* p. 55, col. 1 :—

"The purpose you vndertake is dangerous, the Friends you hane named vncertaine, the Time it selfe vnsorted, and your whole Plot too light, for the counterpoize of so great an Opposition." (L. *oppono,* "to set against, oppose, by way of comparison.")

And in *Cymbeline,* IV., i., 14, where Cloten is contrasting himself with Posthumus :—

"the Lines of my body are as well drawne as his ; no lesse young, more strong, not beneath him in Fortunes, beyond him in the aduantage of the time, aboue him in Birth, alike conuersant in generall seruices, and more remarkeable in single oppositions; yet this imperseuerant Thing loues him in my despight."—First Folio, *Tragedies,* p. 387, col. 1 :—

For here the "single oppositions" is not the plural of the "single opposition," or combat, of the *First Part of King Henry IV.,* I., iii. 99, but of the "opposition" of single qualities in Cloten, and Posthumus, set against one another by way of comparison.

Again, on the word "arrive" (reach), in *Edward III. :—*

"But I will, through a holly spout of blood,
Arrive that Sestos where my Hero lies."

Mr. Swinburne comments,—"Shakespeare, we may observe, does once, but once only, make use of the word 'arrive' in this obsolete active sense. . . . . . .*Julius Cæsar*, Act i., sc. 2." But "sham Shake-speareans" know that the poet used it also in *Coriolanus*, II., iii., 189 :

" And now arriuing
A Place of Potencie, and sway o' th' State."—*Fol.*, p. 13, col. 2.

And in the *Rape of Lucrece*, l. 781 :—

" Ere he arrive his weary noontide prick."

It is also in the *Third Part of King Henry VI.*, V., iii., 8 (probably not Shakspere's) :—

" Those powers that the Queene
Hath rays'd in Gallia haue arriued our coast."—*Fol.*, p. 169, col. 2.

Argal, Shakspere did not write the *First Part of King Henry IV.*, *Cymbeline*, *Coriolanus*, and the *Rape of Lucrece* (as Mr. Swinburne proved last week).

The German scholars whom Mr. Swinburne has treated with such unfairness will be as much amused at his elaborate attempt to teach his grandmother to suck eggs—for his article only comes to the conclusion that Delius, Von Friesen, (and many of us,) had long ago reached—as at his tumbles in the mud during this attempt. We "sham Shakespeareans" shall be content to have exposed the genuine ignorance of the man who has tried to turn Shakspere into a sham, and denied him some of his greatest plays and poems ; and we shall go on quietly with our faithful work.—I am, Sir, &c.,

3 *St. George's Square*, *N.W.*   F. J. FURNIVALL.

P.S.—Among the prior users of the Shaksperean word "rariety " * is the Shaksperean authority, John Florio, in his Englished " Essayes of Lo; Michael de Montaigne," A.D. 1603, —" Report followeth not all goodnesse, except difficulty and *rarietie* be ioyned thereunto." (p. 577; edition 1634.) I need hardly say that a German scholar's book has helped me to expose Mr. Swinburne's " shallow ignorance."

---

* [It is a matter of course that so unscholarlike a person as Mr. Swinburne, who uses as his ultimate authorities his long-ear and a miserable modernisation of Shakspere's text, should go for his spelling of the poet's name to the poet's printer, and not to Shakspere himself. It is also a matter of course that Mr. Swinburne, with his infinite self-conceit, should ridicule those men who *do* try to get at original, manuscript, sources of information, and who prefer " Shakspere's " own signature—which has ne**t**er e after *k*, nor *a* after *e* in the majority of his autographs, and is never written " Shakespeare," while it is thrice written " Shakspere"—to the conceit of his conceit-mongering age which produced the spelling " Shake-speare."]

[On the question at issue between Mr. Swinburne and me on the value of his *ear*, as a measure of SHAKSPERE,—Whether it is a poet's ear, delicate and sufficient for its task, as he conceives it to be, or a poeticule's or poet-aster's ear, too long, hairy, thick, and dull to decide on what are Shakspere's words, as I contend it is,—the evidence in my letters decides. It follows like evidence cited in my former controversy with Mr. Swinburne, when his ear—Bottom's, when translated—declared that there were no triple endings in the Shakspere part of *Henry VIII.*, and that all poets normally used *ignorance* as ~~three~~ syllables, though Milton never does so, &c. This, then, is the second time that the old French proverb, *Il y a ur. Dieu pour les yvrongnes*, has belied itself. Providence has forsaken Mr. Swinburne.]

THE SUCCESSION

OF

SHAKSPERE'S WORKS

&c.

THE SUCCESSION

OF

SHAKSPERE'S WORKS

AND THE USE OF

METRICAL TESTS IN SETTLING IT, &c.

BEING THE INTRODUCTION TO

PROFESSOR GERVINUS'S 'COMMENTARIES ON SHAKSPERE'

TRANSLATED BY MISS BUNNÈTT

(Smith, Elder, & Co., 1877)

BY

FREDK. J. FURNIVALL, M.A.

TRINITY HALL, CAMBRIDGE

Founder and Director of the New Shakspere Society, the Chaucer Society, the Ballad Society, and the Early English Text Society; Honorary Secretary of the Philological Society; Editor of many MSS. and Old Books

LONDON

SMITH, ELDER, & CO., 15 WATERLOO PLACE

1877

INTRODUCTION.

———∘∘⦂⦂∘∘———

'IT IS a disgrace to England, that even now, 258 years after Shakspere's death, the study of him has been so narrow, and the criticism,
however good, so devoted to the mere text and its illustration, and
to studies of single plays, that no book by an Englishman exists which
deals in any worthy manner with Shakspere as a whole, which tracks
the rise and growth of his genius from the boyish romanticism or the
sharp youngmanishness of his early plays, to the magnificence, the
splendour, the divine intuition, which mark his ablest works. The
profound and generous "Commentaries" of Gervinus—an honour to a
German to have written, a pleasure to an Englishman to read—is still
the only book known to me that comes near the true treatment and the
dignity of its subject, or can be put into the hands of the student who
wants to know the mind of Shakspere.' [1]

These words were written by me in the autumn of 1873, when I
founded 'The New Shakspere Society,' and have appeard in that
Society's Prospectus up to this day. Their truth has been confirmd by
all the best judges to whom I have spoken about Gervinus's 'Commentaries' since. One of the ablest of these, my friend Professor
J. R. Seeley—a student of Shakspere from his youth—said, on
returning the book to me, 'The play of *Cymbeline* had always
puzzld me; and now, for the first time, Gervinus has explaind it. I
could not have believd before, that any man could have taught me, at
my time of life, so much about one of Shakspere's plays. It is all
clear now.' In Germany Gervinus's book still holds its ground as the
best æsthetic work on our great poet, and is respected by all thoughtful
men.

My strong conviction of its value leads me, however unworthy for
the task, to say now a few words of recommendation of the book to my
English fellow-students of Shakspere, and to note, for the use of beginners, a few points that may help them in their work: 1. On Gervinus's
book. 2. On the change in Shakspere's metre as he advanct in life,

---

[1] I should now add 'The Mind and Art of Shakspere,' by my friend Professor
Dowden, and my own Introduction to 'The Leopold Shakspere,' Cassell & Co.

and on 'Metrical Tests.' 3. On the spurious portions of plays calld Shakspere's, and the use of metrical tests in detecting them. 4. On noting the progressive changes in Shakspere's language, imagery, and thought. 5. On the succession of Shakspere's plays. 6. On the helps for studying them. I want just to tell a beginner now, what I wish another student had told me when I began to read Shakspere.

§ 1. Most Englishmen who read Shakspere are content to read his plays in any haphazard order, to enjoy and admire them—some greatly, some not much—without any thought of getting at the meaning of them, and at the man who lies beneath them; without any notion of tracing the growth of his mind, from its first upshoot till the ripening of its latest fruits. Yet this is not the way in which the works of SHAKSPERE, the chief glory of English literature, should be studid. Carefully and faithfully is every Englishman bound to follow the course of the most splendid imagination of his land, and to note its purpose in every mark it leaves of its march. Shakspere *must* be studied chronologically, and as a whole. In this task the student will get most real and welcome help from Professor Gervinus. The Professor starts with Shakspere's earliest poems, the *Venus and Adonis*, (full of passion and of Stratford country life), and *Lucrece*, (of which Chaucer's *Troylus* must surely have been the model) ; then reviews his life in London,—wild in its early days,—and the condition of the stage when Shakspere joind it; next, his earliest dramatic attempts, his touchings of *Titus Andronicus* (*Pericles* must be put later), and *Henry VI.*, Part I., and his recast of 2 and 3 *Henry VI.*; with his farces *The Comedy of Errors* and *The Taming of the Shrew.* Then the works of his Second Period, in four divisions: 1. His erotic or love-pieces. 2. His historical plays. 3. His comedies of *The Merry Wives, As You Like It, Much Ado*, and *Twelfth Night.* 4. His Sonnets. Next, the Professor treats the great Third Period of Shakspere's Tragedies, headed by the tragi-comedy *Measure for Measure*, and winding-up with the purposeful and peaceful comedies of later age, *The Tempest* and *Winter's Tale*, and *Henry VIII.*, which (says Mr. Spedding) Shakspere plannd, but wrote less than half of (1,166 lines), Fletcher writing the rest (1,761 lines).

Shakspere's course is thus shown to have run from the amorousness and fun of youth, through the strong patriotism of early manhood, to the wrestling with the dark problems that beset the man of middle age to the time of gloom which weighd on Shakspere (as on so many men) in later life, when, though outwardly successful, the world seemd all against him, and his mind dwelt with sympathy on scenes of faithlessness of friends, treachery of relations and subjects, ingratitude of children, scorn of his kind; till at last, in his Stratford home again, peace came to him, Miranda and Perdita in their lovely freshness and charm greeted him, and he was laid by his quiet Avon's side.

In his last section, ' Shakspeare,' Gervinus sets before us his view of the poet and his works as a whole, and rightly claims for him the highest honour as the greatest dramatic artist, the rarest judge of men and human affairs, the noblest moral teacher, that Literature has yet known.

What strikes me most in Gervinus is his breadth of culture and view, his rightness and calmness of judgment, his fairness in looking at both sides of a question, his noble earnest purpose, his resolve to get at the deepest meaning of his author, and his reverence and love for Shakspere. No one can read his book without seeing evidence of a range of reading and study rare indeed among Englishmen. No one can fail to notice how his sound judgment at once puts the new [1] ' Affaire du Collier,'—the Perkins folio forgeries, &c.,—in its true light; how he rejects the ordinary biographer's temptation—to which so many English Shakspereans yield—of making his hero an angel; how he takes the plain and natural meaning of the ' Sonnets' as their real one, and yet shows us Shakspere rising from his vices to the height of a great teacher of men. No one can fail to see how Gervinus, noble-natured and earnest himself, is able to catch and echo for us the ' still small voice' of Shakspere's hidden meaning even in the lightest of his plays. No Englishman can fail to feel pleasure in the heartfelt tribute of love and praise that the great Historian of German Literature gives to the English Shakspere.

No doubt the book has shortcomings, if not faults. It is German, and occasionally cumbrous; it has not the fervour and glow, or the delicacy and subtlety, of many of Mrs. Jameson's Studies; it does not do justice to Shakspere's infinite humour and fun; it makes, sometimes, little odd mistakes.[2] But still it is a noble and generous

[1] The old forgeries printed by Mr. Collier as genuine were the documents from the Ellesmere (or Bridgwater House) and Dulwich College Libraries, a State Paper, and the latter additions to the Dulwich Letters (see Dr. Ingleby's *Complete View*). I, in common with many other men, have examined the originals with his prints of them. Mr. Collier printed one more name to one document than was in it when produc'd. See Mr. A. E. Brae's opinion at p. 13 of ' Collier, Coleridge, and Shakespeare: a Review, by the Author of "Literary Cookery,"' 1860. None of Mr. Collier's statements should be trusted till they have been verified. The entries of the actings of Shakspere's Plays in Mr. Peter Cunningham's ' Revels at Court' (Shakespeare Society, 1842), pp. 203–5, 210–11, are also printed from forgeries (which Sir T. Duffus Hardy has shown me), though Mr. Halliwell says he has a transcript of some of the entries, made before Mr. Cunningham was born. Thus the following usually relied-on dates are forgd: 1605, *Moor of Venis, Merry Wives, Measure for Measure, Errors, Love's Labours Lost, Henry V., Merchant of Venice*. 1612, *Tempest, Winter's Tale*.

[2] Professor Seeley notices three:—1. In the comment on 1 *Henry IV.* Gervinus takes as literal and serious (p. 309) Hotspur's humourous exaggeration of Mortimer's keeping him *nine hours* listening to devils' names:

> I tell you what:
> He held me last Night *at least nine howres*
> In reckning vp the seuerall Deuils Names
> That were his Lackueyes. (III. i. 155–8, *Folio*, p. 61, col 1.)

book, which no true lover of Shakspere can read without gratitude and respect.

§ 2. Though Gervinus's criticism is mainly æsthetic,[1] yet, in settling the dates and relations of Shakspere's plays, he always shows a keen appreciation of the value of external evidence, and likewise of the metrical evidence, the markt changes of metre in Shakspere's verse as he advanct in life. As getting the right succession of Shakspere's plays is 'a condition precedent' to following the growth of his mind, and as 'metrical tests' are a great help to this end, though they have had, till lately, little attention given to them in England,[2] I wish to say a few words on them.

Admitting (as I contend we must admit) that *Love's Labours Lost* is Shakspere's earliest wholly-genuine play, and contrasting it with two of his latest, *The Tempest* and *Winter's Tale*, we find that— (I.), while in *Love's Labours Lost* the 5-measure ryming lines are 1,028, and the blank verse only 579; in *The Tempest* such ryming lines are 2, and the blank verse 1,458, while in the *Winter's Tale* there are no 5-measure ryming lines to 1,825 blank verse ones. Again, (II.) Shakspere's early blank verse was written on the model of ryming verse, nearly every line had a pause at the end; but as he wrote on, he struggld out of these fetters into a freer and more natural line, which

When Hotspur of course means ten or twelve minutes, or perhaps even five. Certainly poor evidence that Hotspur is patient when in repose, pliable and yielding like a lamb! 2. Gervinus (p. 310) misses the humour of Hotspur's speech to Kate his wife (II. iii. *Folio*, p. 55, col. 2):

> *Hot.* Come, wilt thou see me ride?
> And *when I am a horsebacke*, I will sweare
> I loue thee infinitely,

though he is right in saying Hotspur does love his wife, and that because he banters her. 3. He turns Desdemona's words into Othello's own (p. 517), 'She gave him a "world of sighs;" and she swore (even in remembrance *the Moor deemed it strange and wondrus pitiful*) that she wished she had not heard his story.' Whereas Shakspere says, I. iii. 159-162, *Folio*, p. 314, col. 1:

> She gaue me for my paines a world of [sighs]:
> She swore, in faith, 'twas strange, 'twas strange, 'twas passing strange,
> 'Twas pittifull, 'twas wondrous pittifull:
> She wish'd she had not heard it. . . .

Professor Dowden (who refers to the notice of Gervinus in vol. vi. of the Shakspere *Jahrbuch*) thinks that Gervinus often goes much astray, as in what he says of Mercutio; and that his strong historical tendency imports meanings into the plays which are not there, as when he calls Hamlet a culturd man in an age of rude force, whereas it's an age of Osric, Polonius, universities, &c. The inconsistency, such as it is, seems to me in the facts, and not in Gervinus.

[1] Mr. Halliwell complains of this word being stretcht to include 'psychological and philosophical.'

[2] Malone in 1778 pointed out the value of the Ryme-Test in settling the priority of one early play over another. He also noticed the unstopt or run-on line test, which the late Mr. Bathurst brought more markedly under the notice of modern folk by his little book (1857) on Shakspere's differences of versification.

often ran-on into the next, took the pause from the end, and put it in or near the middle of the line.   Contrast these three extracts:—

LOVES LABOURS LOST, II. i. 13-34.
(*Folio*, p. 120, revised.)

Prin. Good Lord *Boyet*, my beauty, though but mean,
Needs not the painted flourish of your praise.
Beauty is bought by iudgement of the eye,
Not vttred by base sale of chapmens tongues.
I am lesse proud to heare you tell my worth,
Then you much willing to be counted wise,
In spending your wit in the praise of mine.
But now to taske the tasker: good *Boyet*,
You are not ignorant, all-telling fame
Doth noyse abroad, *Nauar* hath made a vow,
Till paineful studie shall outweare three yeares,
No woman may approach his silent Court:
Therefore, to's seemeth it a needfull course,
B fore we enter his forbidden gates,
To know his pleasure, and, in that behalfe,
Bold of your worthinesse, we single you,
As our best mouing faire soliciter.
Tell him, the daughter of the King of France,
On serious businesse crauing quicke dispatch,
Importunes personall conference with his grace.
Haste; signifie so much; while we attend,
Like humble visag'd suters, his high will.

LEAR, IV. iii. 17-25.
(From the *Quarto* of 1608, sig. L 7, ed. Steevens ; *Dyce*, vii. 318, revised.)

Kent.   O then it mou'd her,
Gent. Not to a rage : patience and sorrow stroue
Who should expresse her goodliest. You have seene
Sun-shine and raine at once : her smiles and teares
Were like a better day¹: those happy smilets
That plaid on her ripe lip, seem'd not to know
What guests were in her eyes ; which parted thence
As pearles from diamonds dropt. In briefe, sorrow
Would be a rarity most belou'd, if all
Could so become it.

THE WINTERS TALE, III. ii. 232-243.
Folio, p. 288, col. 1.

Leo.   Thou didst speake but well
When most the truth : which I receyue much bet,ter
Then to be pittied of thee. Prethee, bring me   234
To the dead bodies of my Queene, and Sonne ;
One graue shall be for both. Vpon them shall   [237
The causes of their death appeare (vnto
Our shame perpetuall). Once a day Ile vis|it
The Chappell where they lye ; and teares shed there
Shall be my recrea|tion. So long as Na'ture   240
Will beare vp with this exercise. so long
I dayly vow to vse it.   Come and leade | me   242
To these sorrowes.

¹ Compare *Venus and Adonis*, st. 161, l. 961-6.

The dullest ear cannot fail to recognize the difference between the early *Love's Labours Lost* pause or dwelling on the end of each line, and the later *Lear's* and *Winter's Tale* disregard of it, with (III.) the following shift of the pause to or near the middle of the next line.   In short, the proportion of run-on lines to end-pause ones in three of the earliest and three of the latest plays of Shakspere is as follows:—

Earliest Plays	Proportion of unstopt lines to end-stopt ones	Latest Plays	Proportion of unstopt lines to end-stopt ones
Loues Labour's Lost .	1 in 18·14	The Tempest . . .	1 in 3·02
The Comedy of Errours .	1 in 10·7	Cymbeline King of Bri-taine	1 in 2·52
The Two Gentlemen of Verona . . .	1 in 10	The Winter's Tale . .	1 in 2·12

Again, note that all the above *Love's Labours Lost* lines have only five measures, or ten syllables, each; and not one weak ending, that is, a final unemphatic word, or a word that clearly belongs to the next line, while in *The Winter's Tale* extract there are four lines with extra syllables (240 having one also before the central pause) and three with weak endings, 234, 237, 242. In these points contrast the *Love's Labours Lost* lines also with the two following passages, from *The Winter's Tale*, (Act II., sc. i., l. 158-170; Folio, p. 283), and Shakspere's part of *Henry VIII.* :—

> *Lord.* I had rather you did lacke then I (my Lord)
> Vpon this ground : and more it would content | me   159
> To haue her Honor true, then your suspit|ion,
> Be blam'd for't how you might.
> *Leo.*   Why, what neede we   161
> Commune with you of this? but rather fol|low
> Our forcefull instigation? Our prerog|atiue
> Cals not your Counsailes, but our naturall good|nesse
> Imparts this: which, if you, or stupified,
> Or seeming so, in skill, cannot or will | not
> Rellish a truth, like vs, informe your selues ;
> We neede no more of your aduice : the mat|ter,
> The losse, the gaine, the ord'ring on't, is all
> Properly ours.   (*Winter's Tale*, II. i. 158-170.)

Here (IV.) are seven lines with extra syllables,[1] and (V) two lines, 159, 161, with 'weak-endings,' the coming of which in any number is a sure sign of Shakspere's late work (see the Postscript). Again, take, for the weak ending, *Henry VIII.*, Act III., sc. ii., l. 97-104; Folio, p. 220, col. 2 :—

---

[1] Professor Hertzberg's table of the proportion of 11-syllable lines to all the others (12-syllable and short lines too) in the following 17 plays is given in the Introduction to his German translation of *Cymbeline*, as follows:—

	Per cent.		Per cent.
Love's Labour's Lost . .	4	As You Like It . . .	18
Titus Andronicus . . .	5	Troilus and Cressida . .	20
King John	6	All's Well . . .	21
Richard II. . . .	11·30	Othello	26
Errors	12	Winter's Tale . . .	31·09
Merchant of Venice . .	15	Cymbeline . . .	32
Two Gentlemen . .	15	Tempest . . .	33
Shrew . . .	16	Henry VIII. . . .	44
Richard III. . . .	18		

What though I know her ver|tuous
And well deseruing ? Yet, I know her for   98
A spleeny Lutheran, and not wholsome to   99
Our cause, that she should lye i' th' bosome of   100
Our hard-rul'd King. Againe, there is sprung up
An Heretique. an Arch-one ; *Cranmer*, one
Hath crawl'd into the fauour of the King,
And is his Oracle.

Three weak endings in three consecutive lines, 98–100 ; only one
end-stopt line in 7 ; one with an extra syllable. These are notes of
Shakspere's latest plays ; indeed, his share in *Henry VIII.* was almost
certainly his last work. Or take Mr. Spedding's beautiful instance
from *Cymbeline*, Act IV., sc. ii., l. 220–4 ; Folio, p. 389, col. 1 :—

Thou shalt not lacke
The Flower that's like thy face, Pale Primrose, nor   221
The azur'd Hare-bell, like thy Veines : no, nor   222
The leafe of Eglantine, whom not to slan|der
Out-sweetned not thy breath.

' I doubt whether you will find a single case in any of Shakspere's
undoubtedly early plays of a line of the same structure. Where you
find a line of ten syllables ending with a word of one syllable—that
word not admitting either of emphasis or pause, but belonging to the
next line, and forming part of its first word-group—you have a metrical
effect of which Shakespeare grew fonder as he grew older ; frequent in
his latest period ; up to the end of his middle period, so far as I can
remember, unknown.' (Mr. Spedding's letter to me on his ' Pause-
Test.' ' New Shakspere Soc.'s Trans.,' 1874, p. 31.) Professor W.
A. Hertzberg counts seventy-two weak endings in the 2,407 (omitting
the songs and other lyrical pieces) of *Cymbeline*, or 1 to 33·43, showing
its very late date, 1611 (?) There are other metrical tests, of which
(VI.) the abandonment of doggrel—used only in five plays, all early
or earlyish—and (VII.) the use of 6-measure lines, are two. No one
test can be trusted ; all must be combind and considerd, and us'd as
helps for the higher æsthetic criticism. Every student should work at
these tests for himself.[1] As material that may help him in using the

---

[1] Don't turn your Shakspere into a mere arithmetic-book, and fancy you're a
great critic because you add up a lot of rymes or end-stopt lines, and do a great
many sums out of your poet. This is mere clerk's work ; but it is needed to impress the facts of Shakspere's changes in metre on your mind, and to help others,
as well as yourself, to data for settling the succession of the plays. Metrical tests
are but one branch of the tree of criticism. Mr. Hales's seven tests for the growth
of Shakspere's art and mind in his plays are : 1. External Evidence (entries in the
Stationers' Registers, Diaries, &c.) 2. Historical Allusions in the Plays. 3.
Changes of Metre. 4. Change of Language and Style ; then, Development of
Dramatic Art, as shown in 5. Power of Characterization, and 6. Dramatic Unity.
7. (the most important of all) Knowledge of Life (not only knowledge of its facts,
but a growth of moral insight, and of belief in moral laws ruling men, and the
course of world). See my report of his two Lectures on Shakspere in *The Academy*,
Jan. 17, 1874, p. 63 ; Jan. 31, p. 117.

ryme-test, I reprint from the 'New Sh. Soc.'s Trans.,' 1874, p. 16, Mr. Fleay's 'Metrical Table of Shakespeare's Plays,' though the order of the plays is not rightly given in it—has been since largely alterd by its compiler—and though it has not been verifi'd by any other counter:—

METRICAL TABLE OF SHAKSPERE'S PLAYS.

I. PLAYS OF FIRST (RHYMING) PERIOD.

PLAY.	TOTAL OF LINES.	PROSE.	BLANK.	RHYMES, 5 MEASURES.	RHYMES, SHORT LINES.	SONGS.	DOUBLE ENDINGS.	ALTERNATES.	SONNETS.	DOGGEREL.	1 MEASURE.	2 MEASURES.	3 MEASURES.	4 MEASURES.	6 MEASURES.
Love's L. Lost.	2780	1086	579	1028	54	32	9	236	71	194	4	12	13	—	1
Midsum. N. D.	2251	441	878	731	138	63	29	158	—	—	—	5	3	—	—
Com. of Errors.	1770	240	1150	380	—	—	137	64	—	109	3	8	9	—	—
Rom. and Jul.	3002	405	2111	453	—	—	118	62	28	—	10	20	16	4?	6
Richard II.	2644	—	2107	537	—	—	148	12	—	—	11	17	26	22	33?

II. HISTORIES OF SECOND PERIOD.

PLAY.	TOTAL OF LINES.	PROSE.	BLANK.	RHYMES, 5 MEASURES.	RHYMES, SHORT LINES.	SONGS.	DOUBLE ENDINGS.	ALTERNATES.	SONNETS.	DOGGEREL.	1 MEASURE.	2 MEASURES.	3 MEASURES.	4 MEASURES.	6 MEASURES.
Richard III.	3599	55?	3374	170	—	—	570	—	—	—	20	39	13	23	16
King John.	2553	—	2403	150	—	—	54	12	—	—	1	9	4	4	2
1 Henry IV.	3170	1404	1622	84	—	15	60	4	—	—	16	17	16	16	13
2 Henry IV.	3137	1860	1417	74	7	15	203	[Pistol 64 l.]			3	13	7	—	6
Henry V.	3320	1531	1678	101	2	8	291	[Pist. 157 l.] 14		—	2	13	10	4	23

III. COMEDIES OF SECOND PERIOD.

PLAY.	TOTAL OF LINES.	PROSE.	BLANK.	RHYMES, 5 MEASURES.	RHYMES, SHORT LINES.	SONGS.	DOUBLE ENDINGS.	ALTERNATES.	SONNETS.	DOGGEREL.	1 MEASURE.	2 MEASURES.	3 MEASURES.	4 MEASURES.	6 MEASURES.
T. Gent. of V.	2060	409	1510	116	—	15	203	16	—	18	8	15	32	8	5
Mer. of Ven.	2705	673	1896	93	34	9	297	4	—	4	8	16	22	2	14
Twelf. Night.	2684	1741	763	120	—	60	152	—	—	—	8	21	23	5	10
As you Like it.	2904	1681	925	71	130	97	211	10	—	2	3	10	33	1	5
Merry Wives.	3018	2703	227	69	—	19	32	[Pistol 39 l.]			—	3	3	—	3
Much Ado, &c.	2823	1846	643	40	18	16	129	22	—	—	2	7	15	4	4

IV. COMEDIES OF THIRD PERIOD.

PLAY.	TOTAL OF LINES.	PROSE.	BLANK.	RHYMES, 5 MEASURES.	RHYMES, SHORT LINES.	SONGS.	DOUBLE ENDINGS.	ALTERNATES.	SONNETS.	DOGGEREL.	1 MEASURE.	2 MEASURES.	3 MEASURES.	4 MEASURES.	6 MEASURES.
All's Well.	2981	1453	1234	280	2	12	223	8	14	—	7	31	31	5	14
Meas. for Me.	2809	1134	1574	73	22	5	338	—	—	—	10	29	66	5	47

V. TRAGEDIES OF THIRD PERIOD.

PLAY.	TOTAL OF LINES.	PROSE.	BLANK.	RHYMES, 5 MEASURES.	RHYMES, SHORT LINES.	SONGS.	DOUBLE ENDINGS.	ALTERNATES.	SONNETS.	DOGGEREL.	1 MEASURE.	2 MEASURES.	3 MEASURES.	4 MEASURES.	6 MEASURES.
Troylus and C.	3423	1186	2025	106	—	16	441	—	—	—	10	46	62	13	43
Macbeth.	1993	158	1588	118	129		390	—	—	—	8	28	43	8	13
Cymbeline.	3448	688	2585	107	—	32	726	[84 l. in vision]			8	15	31	18	42
Hamlet.	3924	1208	2490	81	—	60	508	[86 l. in play]			20	53	55	11	47
Othello.	3324	511	2672	86	—	25	646	—	—	—	19	66	71	13	78
King Lear.	3298	903	2238	74	—	83	567	—	—	—	18	34	116	22	50

VI. PLAYS OF FOURTH PERIOD.

PLAY.	TOTAL OF LINES.	PROSE.	BLANK.	RHYMES, 5 MEASURES.	RHYMES, SHORT LINES.	SONGS.	DOUBLE ENDINGS.	ALTERNATES.	SONNETS.	DOGGEREL.	1 MEASURE.	2 MEASURES.	3 MEASURES.	4 MEASURES.	6 MEASURES.
Julius Cæsar.	2440	165	2241	34	—	—	369	—	—	—	14	81	55	6	16
Coriolanus.	3392	820	2521	42	—	—	708	—	—	—	3	33	76	19	42
Antony and C.	3964	255	2761	42	—	6	613	—	—	—	14	38	84	31	61
Tempest.	2068	458	1458	2	—	96	476	[54 l. in masq.]			2	16	47	5	11
Winter's Tale.	2758	844	1825	0	—	57	639	[32 l. in chor.]			8	14	19	13	16

VII. PLAYS IN WHICH SHAKSPERE WAS NOT SOLE AUTHOR.

PLAY.	TOTAL OF LINES.	PROSE.	BLANK.	RHYMES, 5 MEASURES.	RHYMES, SHORT LINES.	SONGS.	DOUBLE ENDINGS.	ALTERNATES.	SONNETS.	DOGGEREL.	1 MEASURE.	2 MEASURES.	3 MEASURES.	4 MEASURES.	6 MEASURES.
Henry VIII.	2754	67?	2613	16	—	12	1195	[46 l. in Prol.			2	19	18	3	32
Two Noble K.	2734	170	2448	54	—	33	1079	& Epilogue].			0	19	46	17	5
Pericles.	2396	418	1436	225	89	—	120	[222 l. Gower].			17	49	59	26	13
Timon of A.	2358	593	1560	184	18	—	257	—	—	—	15	28	54	30	37

VIII. FIRST SKETCHES IN EARLY QUARTOS.

PLAY.	TOTAL OF LINES.	PROSE.	BLANK.	RHYMES, 5 MEASURES.	RHYMES, SHORT LINES.	SONGS.	DOUBLE ENDINGS.	ALTERNATES.	SONNETS.	DOGGEREL.	1 MEASURE.	2 MEASURES.	3 MEASURES.	4 MEASURES.	6 MEASURES.
Rom. and Jul.	2066	261	1451	354	—	—	92	28	—	—	7	26	30	21	92
Hamlet.	2008	509	1462	54	43	—	299	[36 l. in play]			13	45	76	37	30
Henry V.	1672	808	774	30	—	—	104	—	—	—	1	25	35	31	15
Merry Wives.	1395	1207	148	40	38[fairies]	—	10	—	—	—	—	1	—	5	4

IX. DOUBTFUL PLAYS

PLAY.	TOTAL OF LINES.	PROSE.	BLANK.	RHYMES, 5 MEASURES.	RHYMES, SHORT LINES.	SONGS.	DOUBLE ENDINGS.	ALTERNATES.	SONNETS.	DOGGEREL.	1 MEASURE.	2 MEASURES.	3 MEASURES.	4 MEASURES.	6 MEASURES.
T. of Shrew.	2671	516	1971	169	15	—	260	—	—.	49	4	18	22	23	5
Titus Andron.	2525	43	2338	144	—	—	154	—	—	—	4	8	9	9	17
1 Henry VI.	2693	—	2379	314	—	—	140	—	—	—	5	5	4	7	12
2 Henry VI.	3032	448	2562	122	—	—	255	—	—	—	8	25	15	21	12
3 Henry VI.	2904	—	2749	155	—	—	346	—	—	—	13	11	14	11	7
Contention.	1952	381	1571	44	—	—	54	—	—	—	—	14	16	32	44
True Tragedy.	2101	—	2035	66	—	—	148	—	—	—	14	21	29	33	84

That the ryme-test fails to place Shakspere's Plays in their right order, I have shown on pages 32–5 of the 'New Sh. Soc.'s Trans.' 1874 ; but its value, in combination with other tests, is great. Prof. Ingram has tabulated the results of his search with the weak-ending test, so valuable for Shakspere's late plays, and it will be given in my Post-script, p. liv.

§ 3. Besides helping in settling the order of Shakspere's plays, metrical tests give important aid in—1, suggesting, by their differing proportions in different acts, possibly different dates for portions of his genuine plays; and 2, different authors in doubtful plays, and drawing definite lines between spurious and genuine work ; but these tests must never be allowd to override the higher criticism : that must be judge. To take point 2 first. In his undergraduate days at Cambridge (1829–33) Mr. Tennyson pointed out—to Mr. Hallam, among others, who unwisely pooh-poohd the notion — that Fletcher's hand was largely in *Henry VIII*. Later, his friend Mr. James Spedding (the learned and able editor of ' Bacon's Works,' &c.) publisht his working-out of Mr. Tennyson's hint, in an analysis of the play, in ' The Gentleman's Magazine' for August 1850. Mr. Spedding first showd,—by their having markedly the characteristics of Shakspere's style, and the rest of the play not having these ' notes ' of authorship, but having other ' notes ' of Fletcher's hand,—that the scenes below markt Shakspere were his, and those marked Fletcher his.[1] Mr. Spedding then applied the extra-syllable (or feminine-ending) test, and I (in 1873) the end-stopt-line test, with the following result :—

Act	Scene	Lines	Extra Syll.	Proportion.	Author	Unstopt line.
I.	1	225	63	1 to 3·5	Shakspere	1 to 1·83
	2	215	74	,, 2·0	,,	,, 1·86
	3 & 4	172	100	,, 1·7	Fletcher	,, 3·84
II.	1	164	97	,, 1·6	,,	,, 2·96
	2	129	77	,, 1·6	,,	,, 3·43
	3	107	41	,, 2·6	Shakspere	,, 2·37
	4	230	72	,, 3·1	,,	,, 2·13
III.	1	166	119	,, 1·3	Fletcher	,, 4·83
	*2	193	62	,, 3·	Shakspere	,, 2·
	3	257	152	,, 1·6	Fletcher	,, 3·43
IV.	1	116	57	,, 2·	,,	,, 3·
	2	80	51	,, 1·5	,,	} ,, 4·55
	3	93	51	,, 1·8	,,	
	1	176	68	,, 2·5	Shakspere	,, 2·28
V.	2	217	115	,, 1·8	Fletcher	,, 4·77
	3	(almost all prose or rough verse)			,,	,, 5·01
	4	37	44	,, 1·6	,,	,, 6·41

* To exit of the King. The rest of ii. is made iii.

In short, the proportion of Shakspere's double endings,[2] was 1 to

---

[1] Mr. S. Hickson had arrivd before, privately and independently, at the same result. See Prof. Ingram's confirmation on p. liv. *n.* below.

[2] Calld also extra syllables, or feminine endings. Very rarely in Shakspere,

3, of Fletcher's 1 to 1·7; of Shakspere's unstopt lines, 1 to 2·03, of Fletcher's 1 to 3·79, both tests making Shakspere's part of the play his latest work. Mr. Spedding's division of the play between Shakspere and Fletcher was confirmd independently by the late Mr. S. Hickson, in 'Notes and Queries,' ii. 198, Aug. 24, 1850; and by Mr. Fleay in 'New Sh. Soc. Trans.,' 1874, Appendix, p. 23.* It may be lookt on as certain. Again, Mr. Tennyson us't in his undergraduate days to read the genuine parts of *Pericles* to his friends in college. He read them to me in London last December (1873). He pickt them out by his ear and his knowledge of Shakspere's hand. Last April Mr. Fleay sent me, as genuine, the same parts of *Pericles*, got at mainly by working metrical tests. Sidney Walker, Gervinus (nearly), Delius and others, had before attaind the same result. Shakspere wrote the *Marina* story in Acts iii. iv. v., less the brothel scenes and the Gower choruses. These, Rowley wrote, says Mr. Fleay, while G. Wilkins wrote Acts i. and ii. and arrangd the play. ('New Sh. Soc. Trans.,' 1874, p. 195, &c.) Further, the late Mr. Samuel Hickson, in the 'Westminster and Foreign Quarterly' for April 1847, and working after Mr. Spalding and other critics,[1] assignd to Shakspere large part of *The Two Noble Kinsmen*, which was not publisht till 1634, as 'Written by the memorable worthies of the time: Mr. John Fletcher, and Mr. William Shakspeare, Gent.' Mr. Hickson argu'd that Shakspere designd the under-plot as well as the main plot of the play, and wrote Acts I.; II. i.; III. i. ii.; IV. iii. (prose); V. all but scene ii. But I cannot allow that all these are Shakspere's. See my Forewords to the New Sh. Soc., reprint of Professor Spalding's *Letter*. The rest Fletcher wrote, as is shown by its weakness, and its oftener use of the extra final syllable. The double-ending and the end-stopt line tests show that while in the 1,124 supposd Shakspere-lines in the play there are 321 with double endings, that is, 1 in 3·5, and only 1 line of 4-measures, in the 1,398 Fletcher-lines there are 771 with double endings, or 1 in 1·8 (nearly twice as many as in the supposd Shakspere), and 14 lines of 4-measures. Also in the supposd Shakspere's lines the proportion of unstopt lines to end-stopt ones is 1 in 2·41, while in Fletcher's it is 1 in 5·53. See 'Appendix to New Sh. Soc. Trans.,' 1874, where Mr. Spedding's and Mr. Hickson's Papers are reprinted.

Again, the spurious parts of *Timon of Athens* had been more or less completely pointed out by Charles Knight and others. By metrical tests, with some slight help on æsthetic grounds from me, Mr. Fleay has, as I believe, rightly separated the genuine part of the play

---

more frequently in Fletcher, the last syllable is dwelt on:—'Up with a course or two, and tack about, boys.' *Two Noble Kinsmen*, Fletcher, iii., v. 10 (see also ii., ii., 63, 68, 71, 73).

[1] Mr. Tennyson always held that Shakspere wrote much of *The Two Noble Kinsmen*. So did Coleridge, Charles Lamb, and De Quincey. See page lv. below.

from the spurious, except in one instance, and printed it in the 'New Sh. Soc.'s Trans.,' 1874, p. 153–194. Once more, Farmer nearly 100 years ago said that Shakspere wrote only the Petruchio scenes in the *Taming of the Shrew.* Mr. Collier hesitatingly adopted this view. Mr. Grant White develont it, and I (and Mr. Fleay afterwards) turnd it into figures, making the following parts Shakspere's, though in many places they are workt up by him from the old *Taming of a Shrew* :— Induction ; Act II., sc. i., l. 168–326 (? touching 115–167) ; III. ii. 1–125, 151–240 ; IV. i. (and ii. Dyce) ; IV. iii. v. (IV. iv. vi. Dyce) ; V. ii., 1–180 ; in short, the parts of Katharine and Petruchio, and almost all Grumio, with the characters on the stage with them, and possible occasional touches elsewhere. ('New Sh. Soc. Trans.' 1874, 103–110.) The rest is by the alterer and adapter of the old *A Shrew*, possibly Marlowe, as there are deliberate copies or plagiarisms of him in ten passages (G. White).

The Cambridge editors, Messrs. Clark and Wright, have lately opend an attack, in their Clarendon-Press edition, on the genuineness of certain parts of *Macbeth*, and the attack has been inconsiderately developt by Mr. Fleay[1] in the 'New Sh. Soc.'s Trans.,' 1874. So far as the assault is on the Porter's speech, it seems to me a complete failure ;[2] and the notion that a fourth-rate writer like Middleton could have written the grim and pregnant humour of that Porter's speech, I look on as a mere idle fancy. Mr. Hales thinks that the change to the iambic metre in Hecate's speeches, and their inferior quality, point to a different hand, perhaps Middleton's ;[3] but that is all of the play that he or I (who still hesitate[4]) can yet surrender. The wonderful pace at which the play was plainly written—a feverish haste drives it on—will account for many weaknesses in detail. The (probably) after-inserted King's-evil lines are manifestly Shakspere's. Mr. Fleay's late attack on the

[1] See Mr. Hales's excellent Paper on 'The Porter in *Macbeth*' in *The New Sh. Soc. Trans.*, 1874. Also De Quincey on the Knocking, *Works*, xiii. 192–8 ; Furness's *Macbeth*, p. 437.

[2] P.S.—Mr. Fleay's attack on the Porter's speech is now withdrawn. His attempt to make spurious the last three acts of *The Two Gentlemen* has also been wisely withdrawn. His theories, when not confirming former results, should be lookt on with the utmost suspicion.

[3] Middleton is selected, because in his *Witch* (p. 401–2 Furness's *Macbeth*) is a song 'Come away, come away,' which Davenant (who professt to be Shakspere's son by an inn-keeper's wife) inserted in *his* version of Shakspere's *Macbeth* (p. 337, Furness) at the point (III. v. 33) where Shakspere or his editors put *Come away, come away*, in the Folio. Also at the Folio's '*Musicke and a Song. Blacke Spirits.*' IV. i. 43, Davenant inserts Middleton's song 'Black spirits and white, red spirits and gray' (p. 404, p. 339, Furness), with variations.

[4] Compare with the stilted Witch speeches Lucianus's charm-lines in *Hamlet*, III. ii. 266–271. (Consider whether Hamlet's speech for the players of a dozen or sixteen lines (II. ii. 566, III. ii. 1, 86) is III. ii. 197–223, or is never deliverd, as his own excited utterance (III. ii. 272–5), and the King's remorseful rising (276) bring on the crisis which the speech was perhaps intended (III. ii. 86) to provoke. See Prof. Seeley and Mr. Malleson her on, in *N. Sh. Soc. Trans.*, Pt. 2 or 3.

genuineness of parts of *Julius Cæsar* ('New Sh. Soc. Trans.,' 1874, Part 2.) is so groundless, weak and vague, as hardly to deserve mention.

Richard III. has yet to be dealt with. The continuous strain of the women's speeches, and the monotonous 5-measure end-stopt line, have been thought by some to point to a second hand in the play, probably Marlowe's. But Mr. Spedding and I are strongly opposd to this view.

In 1 *Henry VI.* every reader will, I apprehend, see, like Gervinus (p. 101), three hands, though all may not agree in the parts of the play they assign to those hands. Reading it independently, though hastily, before I knew other folks' notions about it, I could not recognise Shakspere's hand till II. iv., the Temple-Garden scene[1] (as Hallam notes). That is all of the play that can be safely assignd to him. I doubt his having written the Suffolk and Margaret love-scene. It so soon falls off.[2] A new ryming man seems to me to begin in IV. vi. vii.; and the first hand seems to write V. ii. iv.,[3] if not all V.

For the argument that Marlowe, Peele, and Greene, wrote *The Contention* and *True Tragedy,*—the foundations of the 2nd and 3rd Parts of *Henry VI.,*—Malone's essay should be consulted. (Variorum ed. of 1821, vol. xviii., p. 555.) On the other side, for the fallacious argument (from the unity of historical view, &c.) that Shakspere wrote all the Three Parts of *Henry VI.,* as well as *The Contention* and *True Tragedy,* Charles Knight's essay in his 'Pictorial Shakspere' (Histories, vol. ii., Library ed. vol. vii.) should be read. For the argument from style, that in lifting or altering 1,479 lines from *The Contention* for

---

[1] This scene has a very large proportion of extra-syllable lines; 30 in 134, or 1 in 4·46. It has 6 run-on lines, or 1 in 22·33. II. ii. 1–15 *may* have a touch of Shakspere, but are probably Marlowe.

[2] Compare l. 28, *Folio,* p. 111, col. 2 :—

> 'Ten thousand French *haue tane the Sacrament*
> To ryue their dangerous Artillerie
> Vpon no Christian soule but English Talbot.'

with *Ric. II.,* V. ii. 17, *Folio,* p. 42, col. 2 :—

> 'A dozen of them heere *haue tane the Sacrament.* . . .
> To kill the King at Oxford.'

[3] Mr. Grant White 'ventures to express the opinion that the greater part of the First Part of *King Henry the Sixth* was originally written by Greene, whose style of thought and versification may be detected throughout the play, beneath the thin embellishment with which it was disguised by Shakspere, and especially in the first and second Scenes of the first Act; that traces of Marlowe's furious pen may be discovered in the second and third scenes of Act II.; and I should be inclined to attribute the couplets of the fifth, sixth, and seventh Scenes of Act IV. to Peele (for their pathos is quite like his in motive, and it must be remembered that Shakespeare has retouched them), were it not that Peele could hardly have written so many distichs without falling once into a peculiarity of rhyme which constantly occurs in his works, and which consists in making an accented syllable rhyme with one that is unaccented.' (Cp. róyal, withál; agó, ráinbow; wáy, Ída; dený, attórney, &c., in 'The Arraignment of Paris.')

Henry VI., Part 2; and 1,931 lines from *True Tragedy* for *Henry VI.*, Part 3, Shakspere was but transferring (but with few exceptions) his own early work to his later recast of these plays, see Mr. R. Grant White's very able essay in his New York edition of Shakspere, vol. vii., p. 403, &c.[1] Mr. Grant White's view certainly goes too far. Marlowe, or one of his school, assuredly helpt in the revision of the early plays. Perhaps a third hand did so too. Miss Jane Lee has in her Paper in the 'New Sh. Soc.'s Trans.,' 1876, given her division of Marlowe's work from Greene's in the *Contention* and *True Tragedy*, and of Shakspere's from Marlowe's in the revising of these plays into *3 & 3 Henry VI.* The reader must carefully work over the ground under Miss Lee's guidance. She assigns to Marlowe's revision, in 2 *Henry VI.* (Globe lines): II. iii. 1–58; III. i. 142–199, 282–330, 357–383; III. ii. 43–121 (with Shakspere); IV. i. 1–147, x. 18–90 (? IV. ix, Greene); V. i. 1–160, 175–195; ii. 10–11, 19–30 (?), 31–65. In 3 *Henry VI.*: I. ii. 5–76; II. i. 81–6, 200–4; ii. 6, 53, 56, 79, 83, 143, 146–8; iii. 49–56; iv. 1–4, 12, 13; v. 114–120; vi. 31–6, 47–50, 58, 100–2; III. iii. 4–43, 47, 48, 67–77, 110–120, 131–7, 141–150, 156–161, 175–9, 191–201, 208–18, 221, 226, 233–8, 244–255 (?); IV. ii. 19–30; V. i. 12–16, 21, 22, 31–3, 39, 48–57, 62–6, 69–71, 78–9, 87–97; iii. i. 24. I should take away even more from Shakspere. See my 'Leopold Shakspere,' Introduction, p. xxxviii.

Titus Andronicus one would only be too glad to turn out of Shakspere's plays, so repulsive are its subject and the treatment of it. But the external evidence is too strong for us.[2] He no doubt retoucht it. He never wrote it. Mr. Wheatley has collected in the 'New Sh. Soc.'s Trans.,' 1874, p. 126–9, the passages in which he thinks he sees Shakspere's hand. See, too, Gervinus, p. 102–6, below.

Act II. of *King Edward III.*, the King's making love to Lady Salisbury, is good enough for a young Shakspere. The metrical evidence shows

---

[1] Mr. R. Grant White's 'opinion is, that the First Part of *The Contention, The True Tragedy*, and probably an early form of the First Part of *King Henry the Sixth.* unknown to us, were written by Marlowe, Greene, and Shakespeare (and perhaps Peele) together .... soon after the arrival of Shakespeare in London; and that he, in taking passages, and sometimes whole Scenes, from those plays for his *King Henry the Sixth* did little more than to reclaim his own' (vii. 407). 'We find, then, that .... Shakespeare retained 2,299 lines of the old version in the new, that he wrote 2,524 lines especially for the new version, and that 1,111 lines of the new version are alterations or expansions of passages in the old. That is, more than three-fourths of the Second and Third Parts of *King Henry the Sixth* may be regarded—with slight allowance for unobliterated traces of his co-laborers—as Shakespeare's own in every sense of the word; and to the remainder he probably has as good a claim as to many passages which he found in prose in various authors, and which were transmuted into poetry in their passage through the magical alembic of his brain.'—R. Grant White, *Shakspeare's Works*, vii. 462.

[2] In the Preface to *Titus* in my big Folio edition you will find a new theory on this subject.—J. O. (Halliwell) Phillipps.

that there are probably two hands in the play ('Academy,' April 25, 1874, p. 462), and the beauty and power of this episode confirm the fact. Moreover, the episode introduces 'two new characters' (Derby and Audley) who 'are afterwards developt after a totally different fashion,' and a third, 'Lodowick, the King's poet-secretary,' who is confind to the episode only. But the episode has nothing to do with the main story of the play: it is not taken from Holinshed's 'Chronicle,' Shakspere's regular authority, but from a collection of novels, Painter's 'Palace of Pleasure,' where it is enlargd (and spoilt) from Froissart. It is unrelievd by the humour shown in the parallel scene of Edward IV. soliciting Lady Elizabeth Grey in 3 *Henry VI.* III. ii.; it is essentially undramatic, except in its last strong situation; and although Shakspere has echoes of it in his works, it is not his. Nor is any other part of the play his. It is certain that Shakspere took no part in the other 'doubtful plays' formerly assignd to him.

We must now hark back to point 1 (p. xxix.), the help that metrical tests give in suggesting or confirming different dates for different periods of a play. This is a question to be approacht with very great caution, and one on which trust in one test may lead to ridiculous absurdities. We have as yet no comparative tables of the differences of metrical peculiarities in the different acts and scenes of Shakspere's plays, nor do we know whether any working test could be got from them if we had. But we do know that Shakspere retouc't and enlargd certain plays, and we are bound to see whether we can recognize in them his later work. *Love's Labours Lost,* for instance, which we feel sure — from its excessive word-play, its prevalence of ryme and end-stopt lines, its large use of doggrel, its want of dramatic development (it is a play of conversation and situation), its faint characterisation, &c. — must have been written quite early, say before 1590, is stated by the Quarto of 1598 (the earliest known) to have been 'Newly corrected and augmented.'[1] So with *All's Well*—

---

[1] I believe that Berowne's last speech in Act III., at least his lines 305-8 in IV. iii., and possibly V. ii. 315-334 (though more in the earlier style) are later insertions. Dyce says on IV. iii. 299-304 (Globe), 312-319 (as compard with 320, &c.), 'Nothing can be plainer than that in this speech we have two passages, both in their original and in their altered shape, the compositor having confounded the new matter with the old.' Mr. Spedding wrote thus on Saturday, Feb. 2, 1839: 'Finished *Love's Labour's Lost.* Observe the inequality in the length of the Acts; the first being half as long again, the fourth twice as long, the fifth three times as long, as the second and third. This is a hint where to look for the principal additions and alterations. In the first Act I suspect Biron's remonstrance against the vow (to begin with) to be an insertion. In the fourth, nearly the whole of the close, from Biron's burst "Who sees the heavenly Rosaline" (IV. iii. 221). In the fifth, the whole of the first scene between Holofernes and Sir Nathaniel bears traces, to me, of the maturer hand, and may have been inserted bodily. The whole close of the fifth Act, from the entrance of Mercade (V. ii. 723), has been probably rewritten, and may bear the same relation to the original

possibly,[1] the recast of *Loues Labours Wonne* (Meres),—*The Merchant of Venice* (in which I agree with Mr. Hales that the casket scenes at least are earlier work), perhaps *Midsummer Night's Dream*, and other plays. And we are bound to search and see whether we can detect any of these augmentations—if not corrections—by their fuller thought and riper style. Study of the parallel-text Quartos will largely help in this.

In the case of *Troilus and Cressida*, as Mr. Alexander J. Ellis (our great authority on Early English and Shaksperean Pronunciation and Metre) said to me, there are clearly three stories: 1. Of Troylus and Cressida. 2. Of Hector. 3. Of Ajax, Ulysses, and the Greek Camp[2]—of which he car'd only to read the third, so far was it above the other two. The point must have been notict often before. To the parts of the play dealing with these three stories, Mr. Fleay has applied the ryme-test, with the following result ('New Sh. Soc. Trans.,' 1874, p. 2), pointing to three different dates for the different parts of the play. That there are two, an early, and a late, I do not doubt; the three dates I do doubt :—

Troylus story	Hector story	Ajax story	
72	50	16	Rhyme lines
607	798	873	Verse lines
1 : 8·4	1 : 13·6	1 : 54·5	ratio

Discussions of the Parliament Scene in *Richard II.*, *All's Well*, *The*

copy which Rosaline's speech " Oft have I heard of you, my Lord Biron," &c. (V. ii. 851-864) bears to the original speech of six lines (827-832), which has been allowed by mistake to stand. There are also a few lines (1-3) at the opening of the fourth Act which I have no doubt were introduced in the corrected copy.

> *Prince.* Was that the king, that spurr'd his horse so hard
> Against the steep uprising of the hill?
> *Boget.* I know not; but I think it was not he.

It was thus that Shakspere learnt to *shade off* his scenes, to carry the action beyond the stage. Thus, in *Romeo and Juliet*, I. ii., old Capulet and Paris enter talking :—

> But Montague is bound as well as I
> In penalty alike, &c.

which was introduced in the amended copy.'

[1] Professors Delius, Hertzberg (who has specially gone into the point), Ingram and Dowden hold that the style, verse, and plot all belong to one period. Craik's and Hertzberg's view that *Love's Labours Wonne* is *The Taming of the Shrew* cannot be supported in the face of the original *Taming of (A) Shrew*.

[2] The Troylus story is in I. i. 1-107, ii. 1-321; II. i. 160, ii.. iii. 1-33; IV. i., ii., iii., iv. 12-53; *IV. v. 277-293; *V. i. 89-93, ii., iii. 97-115, iv. 20-24, v. 1-5, vi. 1-11. (*In all the Act V. scenes, and in IV. v. 277-293, Ulysses or Diomed comes in ; the stories overlap.) The Hector story is in I. i. 108-119, iii. 213-300; II. ii.; III. i. 161-172; IV. iv. 142-150, v. 1-11, 64-276; *V. i., iii. 1-97, v., &c. to the end (except sc. vii. viii. ix., and epilogue, probably spurious). —Fleay. Dyce says, ' That some portions of it, particularly towards the end, are from the pen of a very inferior dramatist, is unquestionable ; and they belong . . . perhaps to the joint production of Dekker and Chettle,' mentioned in Henslowe's *Diary*, p. 147, &c., ed. Shakespeare Soc.

Two Gentlemen (very feeble, as I think), and *Twelfth Night*, are also contained in Mr. Fleay's paper.

§ 4. As Shakspere's change of metre was but one of the signs of the growth of his art and power, the student must watch for all further manifestations of that growth in the poet's work; daring use of words, crowding new and fuller meanings into them, so as often to produce obscurity (specially in *Macbeth* and *Lear*[1]); change from fancy to imagination in figures of speech; increase in power of making his characters live, so that they become real men and women to you; deepening of purpose; heightening of tone; broadening of view; the insight growing greater as the art became perfect. To this end, registers should be made of all peculiar phrases, happy uses of words, and striking metaphors in the plays, as successively read; the parallel-texts of the first and second Quartos of *Romeo and Juliet* (now in the press for the New Sh. Soc., edited by Mr. P. A. Daniel), of *Hamlet* (edited by Josiah Allen, with preface by Samuel Timmins; Sampson Low, 1860), and other plays, when publisht, should be compard. Shakspere's treatment of the same thought or subject at different periods of his life should also be compard; take, for instance, the pretty impatience of Juliet to get news of Romeo out of her nurse in *Romeo and Juliet*; of Rosalind to get news of her lover, Orlando, out of Celia, in the later *As You Like It*; and of Imogen to get tidings of her husband, Posthumus, out of Pisanio, in the still later *Cymbeline*, III., ii. Again, the separation in storm and shipwreck of the family of Ægeon, and the re-union of father, child, and mother in the early *Comedy of Errors*, should be compard with the nearly-like re-union, if not separation, in the much later *Pericles*, &c. For incidents, take Mr. Spedding's happy instance of Shakspere's treatment of the face of a beautiful woman just dead:

1. *Romeo and Juliet*, second edition (1599), not in the first edition, therefore presumably written between 1597 and 1599:—

> Her blood is settled, and her joints are stiff.
> Life and these lips have long been separated.
> *Death lies on her, like an untimely frost*
> *Upon the fairest flower of all the field.*

2. 'Antony and Cleopatra' (1608, according to Delius, &c.):—

> If they had swallow'd poison, 'twould appear
> By external swelling: *but she looks like sleep,*
> *As she would catch another Anthony*
> *In her strong toil of grace.*

3. 'Cymbeline' (date disputed, but *I* say one of the latest [? 1611 plays) :—

> How found you him? [Imogen disguis'd as a youth.]
>   Stark, as you see,
> *Thus smiling, as some fly had tickld slumber,*
> *Not as death's dart being laughd at.* His right cheek
> Reposing on a cushion.

---

[1] Mr. Hales, in *Academy*, Jan. 17, 1874, p. 63, col. 3.

'The difference in the treatment in these three cases represents the progress of a great change in manner and taste : a change which could not be put on or off like the fashion, but was part of the man ' ('New Sh. Soc.'s Trans.,' 1874, p. 30). Beautiful as the tender pathos of the first image, Fancy-bred, is, we must yet feel that in the second and third the Imagination of the poet dwells no longer on the outside, but goes to the very heart of the matter. Cleopatra is shown in the deepest desire of her life; Imogen in her purity smiling unconsciously at death.[1]

Of stage situations and business, Shakspere started with a perfect mastery : his first two plays, *Love's Labours Lost* and *Errors*, prove

---

[1] Compare, in Mr. Ruskin's chapter "Of Imagination Penetrative," 'Modern Painters,' Vol. II., Part II., § 2, Chap. III., p. 158, ed. 1848, his instance of lips described by Fancy, dwelling on the outside, and Imagination going to the heart and inner nature of everything. The bride's lips red (Sir John Suckling); fair Rosamond's, struck by Eleanor (Warner); the lamp of life, 'as the radiant clouds of morning through thin clouds' (Shelley); and then the bare bones of Yorick's skull (*Hamlet* V. i. 207):—

'Here hung those lips that I have kissed, I know not how oft! Where be your gibes now? your gambols? your songs? your flashes of merriment, that were wont to set the table on a roar?'

'There is the essence of life, and the full power of imagination.

'Again compare Milton's flowers in *Lycidas* with Perdita's (in the *Winter's Tale*). In Milton it happens, I think generally, and in the case before us most certainly, that the imagination is mixed and broken with fancy, and so the strength of the imagery is part of iron and part of clay :—

    'Bring the rathe primrose, that forsaken dies, (*Imagination*)
    The tufted crow-toe and pale jessamine, (*Nugatory*)
    The white pink and the pansy freak'd with jet, (*Fancy*)
    The glowing violet, (*Imagination*)
    The musk rose and the well-attir'd woodbine, (*Fancy, vulgar*)
    With cowslips wan that hang the pensive head, (*Imagination*)
    And every flower that sad embroidery wears.' (*Mixed*)

'Then hear Perdita :—

                ' O, Proserpina,
    For the flowers now, that frighted thou let'st fall
    From Dis's waggon. Daffodils,
    That come before the swallow dares, and take
    The winds of March with beauty. Violets, dim,
    But sweeter than the lids of Juno's eyes,
    Or Cytherea's breath. Pale primroses
    That die unmarried, ere they can behold
    Bright Phœbus in his strength, a malady
    Most incident to maids.'

'Observe how the imagination in these last lines goes into the very inmost soul of every flower, after having toucht them all at first with that heavenly timidness, the shadow of Proserpine's, and gilded them with celestial gathering; and never stops on their spots or bodily shapes; while Milton sticks in the stains upon them, and puts us off with that unhappy freak of jet in the very flower that, without this bit of paper-staining, would have been the most precious to us of all. 'There is pansies: that's for thoughts.' (Ophelia, in *Hamlet*.)

it, and his undoubtedly prior training as an actor,[1] render it probable ; but in characterization his growth from *Loves Labours Lost* to *Henry IV.* was wonderfully rapid and sure. Much higher than that he could not grow, though he could spread his branches over all the earth. In knowledge of life he increast to the end ;[2] in wisdom he ripend ; leaving his works to us, a joy and possession for ever.

§ 5. These works I would have the student read in the following order, setting aside *Titus Andronicus* (quite early) and *Henry VI.* (recast before *Henry IV.*), till he is able to judge of them for himself. And as he reads, I would have him notice how Shakspere's successive plays throw out tendrils round those on each side of them,[3] and become linkt together, and how Shakspere himself grows under his studier's eyes, not only changing in the metrical points noticed on p. xxiv.-xxvii. above, but also in all the high and deep qualities of his nature, mentioned on p. xxxvi. The whole man mov'd together—word, mind, and spirit too ; and, to go back to the metaphor above,

> This royal tree hath left us royal fruit,
> Which, mellowd by the stealing hours of time,

will be doubly enjoyd, in its ripeness, by the student who has watcht it from its blossom in the spring.

Shakspere began his dramatic career with Fun, with quizzing some of the absurd fashions of his day, holding ' the mirror up to nature,' showing ' virtue her own feature, scorn her own image, and the very age and body of the time his form and pressure.' (*Hamlet*, III. ii. 24-7.) In *Love's Labours Lost*—a play almost without a plot—he ridicul'd the nonsensical euphuism of his day, the empty affectations of the London wits, and a scheme for shutting out women from men-students' society, as Tennyson did the converse in his ' Princess,' in 1847. He put into this play his Stratford outdoor life and rough country acting ; got a good deal of fun out of the mistaking of one person for another (which is one of the links between his first three plays, each being a Comedy of Errors); and made, as he so often after-wards did, a woman the leader and teacher of men. This *Love's Labours Lost* is full of crackers of word-play and puns. In his second

---

[1] Though the earliest print of Shakspere's name as an actor is 1594 (found by Mr. Halliwell), yet Mr. R. Simpson's quotations about ' feathers ' in *The Academy*, April 4th, 1874, p. 368, col. 2, show that Greene, when calling Shakspere an upstart crow ' beautified with our feathers ' (G.'s *posthumus Groatsworth of Wit*, 1592) meant to speak of him as an actor, and evidently then a well-known one, as well as an author. In 1598 Shakspere acted in Ben Jonson's ' Every Man in his Humour:' see p. 72 of this comedy in Jonson's *Works*, 1616.

[2] Mr. Hales, in *Academy*, Jan. 17, 1874, p. 63, col. 3.

[3] Each play has, in fact, a set of hooks-and-eyes of special pattern on each side of it ; and, when its place is found, its hooks-and eyes will be found to fit into the eyes and-hooks of the plays next it.

play, *The Comedy of Errors*, he took his farcical plot from Plautus, and added to it the pathetic background of old Ægeon's search for his sons, and threatend death, with the first upspringing of earnest, tender love of one Antipholus for Luciana. He dealt, too, with the relation of man and wife in a happily-past tone. The play is a roaring farce, full of capital situations. Then, in *Midsummer Night's Dream*, Shakspere took an immense shoot forward, wedded the loveliest, most delicate fancy of fairyland[1] to Stratford clowndom, and first reveald a genius able to reach to any height. This is specially his Stratford play, full of out-door life and country lore. But it's a dream (as he calls it), or poem, rather than a play, and is disfigur'd by its heroines' quarrels—one's long legs, and the other's sharp temper and nails. In his fourth play Shakspere fell back in power, though he advanc't in dramatic construction. He now first chose his subject from Italy— that Italy which so taught Chaucer and the Western world—and in *The Two Gentlemen of Verona* got hold of that quick, versatile, passionate Southern nature that was hereafter to stand him in such good stead. The play is interesting chiefly as its writer's first drama, as containing his second comic creation—Launce—Bottom being the first, and as preparing the way, by its banisht Valentine, for *Romeo and Juliet*. Love and its vagaries, of the early plays, stop here; Passion follows. (The *Two Gentlemen* is very weak in the latter part; and, in its Valentine's willingness to surrender Sylvia, offends every reader.) In his next play, and poems, Shakspere again takes another enormous shoot forward. Passion is his theme now; lawful in his play, unlawful in his poems. The fresh young figure of Juliet, 'clad in the beauty of the' Southern spring, steps from her winter home, for just two days and nights, into the light and warmth of summer sun, and then sinks into the chill and horrors of the charnel-house and the grave, leaving you under the witchery of her Cenci eyes, that follow you sadly, wistfully, wander where you will. Young and poor as much of the play is, it is yet 'a joy for ever.' With it must be read Shakspere's first poem. *Venus and Adonis* (1592-3) has all the lovely fancy—and the fancy badly-turnd conceit—of *Romeo and Juliet*: and it has the latter's passion, tho' unlawful, repulsive here. I can't help thinking that Shakspere was askt by Lord Southampton to take the subject, and then, through the close, hot atmosphere of heathen lust, he blew the fresh cool breezes and scents of English meads and downs.[2] *Lucrece* (1593-4) is the story of Tarquin's lust. The pure image of the chaste Lucrece asleep—to be set by that of Imogen in *The Winter's Tale* of

---

[1] Possibly, part of this is of a later date than the framework of the play.

[2] In the 'Venus' it is not only the well-known descriptions of the horse (l. 260-318), and the hare-hunt (l. 673-708), that show the Stratford man, but the touches of the overflowing Avon (72), the two silver doves (366), the milch doe and

1611[1]—is one of the triumphs of Shakspere's early time. The long complaints after the Rape are quite in the manner of Troilus in the 4th and 5th books of Chaucer's poem, and I cannot doubt that Shakspere here follow'd 'my maister Chaucer.' Possibly, too, at this time he wrote the Troilus and Cressid part of his later play; and I wish I could add that he balanced it by the king-and-countess episode in *Edward III.* (see p. xxxiii. above), with its pure and noble English woman and wife, Lady Salisbury. But, notwithstanding Mr. Tennyson's dictum in favour of its genuineness, I cannot accept this act as Shakspere's. Before or about this time Shakspere turned to English History. Burning questions of the day were around him; subjects in plenty at hand to let him speak through, what, as an Englishman who lovd his land, he had to say. Elizabeth was accus'd of being under the thumb of favourites; her deposition was plotted; she herself said to Lambarde, 'I am Richard II. Know you not that?' her right to the Crown was disputed; foreign interference was calld for; the Pope appeald to. On these topics Shakspere spoke. He took first the weak English kings, *Richard II., Henry VI.,* and *John.*[2] Or grant, if you will, that he didn't take them, that *Henry VI.* was put into his hands to revise; that *Richard II.* and *John* were orderd by old Burbage; or that some one saw they'd make good plays. Yet Shakspere spoke, and said that government by favourites, quarrels among nobles, ruind a kingdom, lost its possessions (the loss of Calais in 1558 many of his hearers could remember in 1592–4); that rebels who calld-in foreign helpers *must* be betrayed by them; but that if the nation would unite,

> Come the three corners of the world in arms,
> And we shall shock them. Nought shall make us rue,
> If England to itself do rest but true.

While to the Pope, who backt the Armada of 1588, he sent the English message,

> that no Italian priest
> Shall tithe or toll in our dominions.
> *King John,* III. i. 153–4.

---

fawn in somo brake in Charlecote Park (875–6), the red morn (453), of which the weatherwise say:—

> 'A red sky at night's a shepherd's delight;
> A red sky at morning's a shepherd's warning;'

the hush of the wind before it rains (458), the many clouds consulting for foul weather (972), the night owl (531), the lark (853), &c. &c.; just as the artist (289) and the shrill-tongued tapsters (849) show the taste of London life.—F. J. F., in 'The Academy,' Aug. 15, 1874, p. 179, col. 1.

[1] Note the contrast of treatment, as in all cases of early and late handling of a like subject.

[2] The strong *Richard III.* was interpolated, to complete the *Henry VI.* series.

Looking at the historical plays only as dramas, one sees what a splendid subject Shakspere had in *Henry VI.*, and one regrets that he didn't rewrite the four plays on it (I count *Richard III.* as one of them). The old love of Guinevere and Lancelot, with all its sad accompaniment of ruin of Arthur's noble fellowship, was again seen in Margaret and Suffolk. The 'fairest beauty, tender,' soft as 'downy cygnets' (1 *Hen. VI.* V. iii. 46–57) is turnd by ambition, and then by loss of love, and child, and throne, into a 'she-wolf of France,' but worse than wolves of France, a demoness of the French Revolution,

> Whose tongue more poisons than the adder's tooth.

The noble Glo'ster, whom in her pride she murderd, who was the chief pillar of her throne, by his fall let work all the eating passions of the nobles, the schemes of the crafty Richard, that soon bring the Queen and her weak and flabbily-pious Henry to the ground. The figure of Richard rises, chuckling in his villainy and success. But behind him is the gathering storm of Margaret's, Anne's, Elizabeth's curses, the wail of murdered innocents mixt with the women's wrath; and at last the storm bursts, with lightning flash, on the villain's head, on him, erect, defiant, dreading death as little as he feared sin. What could not Shakspere have made of this, with Third-Period power? Another element of effect, too, is the noble Talbot's death, with his gallant son's. Poor as the First Part is, messt about by divers hands, we yet have Nash's witness how it toucht the Elizabethans.[1] Among Shakspere's additions in Parts II. and III. to *The Contention* and *True Tragedy*, are the fine speeches of Duke Humphrey, 'Brave peers,' I. i.; the recast of the Cade scenes, IV. ii.–viii., in Part 2; and Henry's reflection speech in II. v., in Part 3.

Richard III. is written in the manner of Marlowe,[2] Shakspere's only rival; no doubt one of the authors of *The Contention* and *True Tragedy.* Marlowe embodied a passion as his hero,—Ambition in Tamburlaine, Avarice in Barabas, the Love of Knowledge in Faustus,— and sacrifict the gradation of Nature to the one glaring hue he had chosen for his chief character. Richard III. and Iago are Shakspere's only figures in this style. In *Richard III.* the figure of the king is the whole picture, or nearly so; and, striking though that figure is in its deliberate, exultant, scornfully humourous villainy and hypocrisy, we yet feel that the play as a drama suffers from the want of balance in

[1] How would it have joy'd brave Talbot (the terror of the French) to thinke that after he had lyne two hundred yeare in his tomb he should triumph againe on the stage, and have his bones new embalmed with the teares of ten thousand spectators at least (at severall times), who, in the tragedian that represents his person, imagine they behold him fresh bleeding.—*Pierce Penilesse* (1592), p. 60, ed. 1842, Sh. Soc.

[2] He was the son of a cobbler, or parish-clerk, at Canterbury; later, M.A. of St. John's College, Cambridge, and stabd in a tavern brawl in 1593, aged 29.

it. The monotony of the cursing, the weakness of the citizens-scene, the large proportion of extra-syllable lines (570, more than in *Hamlet* or *Lear*), the want of relief in the play, have led many to suspect an underlying hand in it, as in 2 and 3 *Henry VI.* Having once thought this possible, if not likely, I now give it up.

Richard II. is a better balanct play than *Richard III.*, but less powerful in conception and working-out; very weak in its later rymed scenes, and showing an odd absence of Shakspere's specialty of characterization in the gardener, who talks like a philosopher, or Friar Lawrence in *Romeo and Juliet*: sermons in plants they both find. There is no mixture of comedy in the play, and no prose, as in *John.* The character of the sham, clap-trap king, claiming the attributes of royalty when its reality is no longer within him, affecting—the idiot!— to honour England's earth by touching it with his hand; indulging in tall talk like Hamlet, and then directly eating his big words; up to the heavens in one speech, and down to the dust in the next,—is well brought out. Yet at last his weaknesses are hid, his sins against his land well nigh forgiven, under the veil of pity for his end that Shakspere throws over Richard's corpse. In Gaunt's speech on England (II. i. 40–68) Shakspere the patriot speaks to us and all Englishmen to the end of time. And sad it is to think that we Victorians have to repeat his protest still, and say that in the support of the empire of Sodom, the misrule that suffers, and rewards the perpetrators of, the direst savageries this age has heard of,—in the support of this for 'English interests' (or the devil's?), this 'dear, dear land' of ours

> ' is now bound in with shame,
> With inky blots and rotten parchment bonds.
> That England, that was wont to conquer others,
> Hath made a shameful conquest of itself.'

King John, the play of pathos and patriotism, is linkt strongly to *Richard II.* and *Richard III.*, but is a great advance on them. It is founded on, and follows, the earlier play of *The Troublesome Raigne* of King John, and should be read carefully with it, to see the change that genius has made in poorer work. The old outlines are mainly left, but the glory of colour is new. The hands are Esau's hands, but the voice is the voice of Jacob. Unluckily, Shakspere left the guidance of the old play which connects the poisoning of John with his opposition to the Pope and his plundering the abbeys, and thus laid his drama open to the objection that its climax has nothing to do with its motive or action. And he did this in spite of one story in Holinshed which justified the connection. But the passionate love and yearning of Constance for her boy, which no one who has lost a child can ever forget; the pathos of young Arthur's appeal for his life, and then his death; the lift, by it, of the rough Faulconbridge from his professt following of gain as God, into true nobility and gentleness of soul: these make *King John* a truly memorable play. After it Shakspere shone forth in full power in *The Merchant*, whence Shylock's curses, Portia's plea for mercy, Gratiano's humour, the Gobbos' farce, rise in harmony with the song of heaven's own choir of stars. He next perhaps re-wrote the amusing Petruchio-Katharine-Grumio scenes in *The Taming of the Shrew*, with its racy Induction. In his three comedies of Falstaff, or the First and Second Parts of *Henry IV*. and the *Merry Wives*,[1] he culminated in humour and comic power.[2] Never equalld has Falstaff been, and never will be, I believe. The drama of Shakspere's hero, *Henry V.* (in 1599),[3] then closd the connected series of his historical plays,[4] with its splendid bursts of patriotism—possibly against

---

[1] The *Merry Wives* was a piece hastily written to please Queen Elizabeth: so says tradition; and rightly, I believe. No doubt it was revis'd; but for intrinsic merit it cannot stand for a moment by *Henry IV*.

[2] *Henry IV.*, or at least the First Part of it, must have been written in or about 1597, the proudest year of Shakspere's early life, when, not quite thirty-three, he bought New Place, 'the great house' of Stratford.

[3] In 1599 also, Shakspere became a partner in some of the profits of the Globe. See the "Memorial of Cutbert Burbage, and Winifred his brother's wife, and William his sonne," in 1635, to the Lord Chamberlaine, discovered by Mr. J. O. Halliwell in 1870, made public by him in 1874, printed by me from the Record Office MS. in *The Academy*, March 7, and since issued privately by Mr. Halliwell. 'The father of us, Cutbert and Richard Burbage, was the first builder of playhowses, and was himselfe in his younger yeeres a player. "The theater" hee built with many huundred poundes taken up at interest. The players that lived in those first times had only the profitts arising from the dores; but now the players receave all the commings in at the dores to themselves, and halfe the galleries from the houskepers [the owners or lessees of the theatre]. Hee built this house upon leased ground, by which meanes the landlord and hee had a great suite in law, and, by his death, the like troubles fell on us his sonnes: wee then bethought us of altering from thence, and at like expence built the Globe [A.D. 1599: Mr. Halliwell says] with more summes of money taken up at interest, which lay heavy on us many yeares; *and to ourselves wee joyned those deserving men, Shakspere, Hemings, Condall, Philips, and others, partners in the profittes of that they call the House.* . . .

'Thus, Right Honorable, as concerning the Globe, where wee ourselves are but lessees. Now for the Blackfriers: that is our inheritance; our father purchased it at extreame rates, and made it into a playhouse with great charge and trouble: which after was leased out to one Evans that first sett up the boyes commonly called the Queenes Majesties Children of the Chappell. In processe of time, the boyes growing up to bee men, which were Underwood, Field, Ostler, and were taken to strengthen the King's service; and the more to strengthen the service, the boyes dayly wearing out, it was considered that house would bee as fitt for ourselves, and soe [we] purchased the lease remaining from Evans, with our money, and placed *men players, which were Hemings, Condall, Shakspeare,' &c.* This could not have been till, or after the year 1603, when James succeeded Elizabeth, and there was a 'King's service.' Besides, the Warrant of King James making Shakspere's company the King's Company, and which bears date May 17th, 1603, mentions only the Globe, as this Company's ' now usuall house.'

[4] *Henry VIII.*, not part of the series, was added at the end of Shakspere's life. See Mr. Richard Simpson's able Paper on the 'Politics of Shakspere's Historical

the contemporary glorification of the great Henri Quatre of France—though they cannot save the play from its weakness as a drama, necessitated by a battle (Agincourt) standing for its plot. It was succeeded by a brilliant set of comedies, possibly for the newly-opend Globe theatre:— *Much Ado about Nothing* (glittering with stars of wit and richest humour:—what do not the names Benedick and Beatrice, Dogberry and Verges mean to a Shakspere-reader's ear?); *As You Like It* with its moral, 'Sweet are the uses of adversity,' its freshness of greenwood life, wherein men 'fleet the time carelessly as they did in the golden world'; and yet with its melancholy Jaques, who will not be comforted or glad, a prelude to the sadder time so close at hand. *Twelfth Night* (with its pompous goose of a Malvolio, its sharp Maria, its drunken Toby Belch and Andrew Aguecheek, its Viola with her beautiful self-sacrificing love for the Duke). *All's Well* (the recast of *Love's Labours Wonne*), with its unpleasant plot of a willing wife (Helena, one of Shakspere's noblest ladies) hunting and catching her unwilling husband, but with its inimitable braggart Parolles.

Here Shakspere's 'Sonnets' should be read, and the tender sensitive nature that produced them commund with. Over and over again must they be read, till at least their main outlines are clear. The key to them is No. cxliv. on 'the man right fair,' who is the poet's 'better angel,' and 'the worser spirit a woman colour'd ill.' They clearly speak of Shakspere's own loves and life, and interpret his plays. The later 'Sonnets' are the best preparation for *Hamlet*.

Undoubtedly at this time a shadow of darkness fell upon Shakspere. What causes brought it, we cannot certainly tell. Private reasons the 'Sonnets' show. He was deserted by his mistress—wrongly but madly lovd by him, in spite of the struggles of his better nature—for his dearest friend; and this for a time severd their friendship, never to be restord again as it first was. Public reasons there were: his great patron and friend Southampton[1] was declard traitor and imprisond in 1601; was threatend with death, and in almost

Plays' in *The New Shakspere Soc.'s Trans.*, 1874 or -5. He argues 'that Shakspere was of the Essex party, against Burghley and Cecil; that in *Henry VI.* and *Richard II.* he showd Elizabeth misled by Leicester, and then by Burghley (she herself said she was Richard II.); that *John* was aimd at the many callers for foreign invention in her time, his wars were hers of 1585; *Henry IV.* showd how she us'd and cast off helpers, and picturd the Northern Rebellion in her reign (1569); *Henry V.* told her how foreign war united a nation, and brought about religious toleration at home (this was Essex's policy); *Henry VIII.* brought out the end of the constantly falling state of the old nobility, (which Shakspere, in common with so many Elizabethans, lamented,) and the consummation of the full power of the Crown, two threads running through English history and Shakspere's Historical Plays. Shakspere's changes of the Chronicles were not only for dramatic effect, but to show the lessons he wisht them to teach on the political circumstances of his time.'

[1] This is Gervinus's suggestion. In the dedication to *Lucrece*, Shakspere says to Southampton, 'The love I dedicate to your lordship is without end.'

daily danger of it till Elizabeth's own death in 1603 set him free
through King James: the rebellion and execution of Essex, Southampton's friend and the cause of his ruin, to whom Shakspere had two
years before alluded with pride in his Prologue to *Henry V.*, Act v.
1. 30. At any rate, the times were out of joint. Shakspere was
stirrd to his inmost depths, and gave forth the grandest series of
Tragedies that the world has ever seen: *Julius Cæsar*, *Hamlet* (followd
by the tragi-comedy *Measure for Measure*), *Othello*, *Macbeth*, *Lear*,
Troilus and Cressida (see p. **xxxv.**), *Antony and Cleopatra*, *Coriolanus*, *Timon*; showing what subjects were then kin to his frame of
mind; how he felt, and struggld with, the stern realities of life; how
he dwelt on the weakness and baseness of men, their treachery as friends
and subjects, their lawless lust and ungovernd jealousy as lovers, their
serpent-like ingratitude as children, their fickleness and disgustfulness
as the many-headed mob, fit only to be spit upon and curst: over all
he held the terrors of conscience and the avenging sword of fate. All
had 'judgment here.'

But Shakspere could not end thus. After the darkness came light;
after the storm, calm; and in the closing series of his plays—three
tragedies, two comedies, and one history—inspird, I believe, by his
renewd family-life at Stratford[1]—he speaks of reconciliation and peace.
His Tragedies now, for the first time, end happily; his Comedies have
a quite new fulness of meaning and love; his History (though partly
by Fletcher's mouth) speaks an injurd wife's forgiveness of deepest
wrongs, and prophesies blessings. All the plays turn on broken family
ties united, or their breach forgiven unavengd. With wife and daughters
again around him, the faultful past was rememberd only that the present
union might be closer. In *Pericles* (see p. **xxx.**) the bereavd king
finds once more his lost daughter, whose supposd death had made him
dumb; then both are united to the wife-and-mother whose seeming
corpse had been committed to the waves; and the rush of joy at their
at-onement sweeps away all thought of vengeance on their enemies.
Again, in *The Tempest*—wherein Shakspere 'treads on the confines of
other worlds'—wherein his new type of Stratford maiden is idealizd
into Miranda, 'so delicately refind, all but ethereal, in her virgin innocence' (Mrs. Jameson),—his lesson is still of the breaking of family
ties—brother and brother—repented of and forgiven:—

> The rarer action is
> In virtue than in vengeance: they, being penitent,
> The sole drift of my purpose doth extend
> Not a frowne further.—V. i. 27–30; *Fol.* p. 16, col. 2.

---

[1] Unless Thomas Greene, the Town Clerk of Stratford, was living at New
Place with his 'cosen Shakspere' or his family, Shakspere cannot well have retired
thither till after September 1609, as Greene then said a G. Brown might stay

In his next play, *Cymbeline*, he again proclaims to the repentant sinner his Fourth Period message,

> The power that I have on you is to spare you;
> The malice towards you, to forgive you . . . .
> Pardon's the word for all.

While, as regards family life, he makes the true wife Imogen—'the most perfect' Imogen—wrongly and hastily mistrusted, rise from desertion and seeming death, to forgive and clasp to her ever-loving heart the husband who had doubted her: no Desdemona end for her.[1] Reiterating his lesson, Shakspere gives us again, in his last complete play, the delightsome *Winter's Tale*, the noble wife, Hermione, calm in her dignity, saintlike in her patience, forgiving her basely jealous and vindictive husband, while he unites them again—as in *Pericles*—with their lost daughter Perdita, sweet with the fragrance of her Stratford flowers of spring, artless and beautiful, tender and noble-naturd, as Shakspere alone could make her. In his fragments, completed by other smaller men, the teaching is still the same. In *The Two Noble Kinsmen*, he shows us the forsworn brother (Arcite) dying repentant, recommending his brother (Palamon) to Emelye, his first love. In *Henry VIII.*, Katharine the divorced, pious, affectionate, simple, magnanimous,—in one sense, 'the triumph of Shakespeare's genius and his wisdom' (Mrs. Jameson, pp. 379, 384)—forgives her ruffian husband 'all, and prays God to do so likewise':—

> tell him, in death I blest him,
> For so I will.   Mine eyes grow dimme: Farewell.—*Fol.* p. 226.[2]

---

longer in his house, 'the rather because I perceyved I might stay another yere at New Place.' By June 21, 1611, Thomas Greene is probably in his new house, as an order was made that the town is 'to repare the churchyard wall at Mr. Greene's dwelling place.'—Halliwell's *Hist. of New Place.*

[1] Note, too, how, in *Cymbeline*, Shakspere contrasts the evils of court life with the simplicity and innocence of country life, life then around him, as I contend.

[2] Note that in *Henry VIII., Cymbeline,* and *Winter's Tale* (group *b*) the forgiveness is mainly by women, in *Pericles* and *The Tempest* (group *a*), by men, while in four of these plays you have the additional link of lost children restored to their parents. Contrast this link with that of fun from mistaken identity in the first three First-Period Plays, *L. L. Lost, Errors, Dream.* Between this first group, and the second or Passion one, of *Romeo & Juliet, Venus,* and *Lucrece,* the *Two Gentlemen* serves as a link. The Second Period Plays fall into *a.* a Life-Plea group, *John,* and *The Merchant* ; *b.* the *Shrew* ; *c.* the Three Comedies of Falstaff, with the Trilogy of *Henry IV., V.*; *d.* the three Sunny or Sweet-Time Comedies, *Much Ado, As You Like It, Twelfth Night* ; *e.* the Darkening Comedy, *All's Well.* The Third Period Plays fall into five groups: *a.* the Unfit-Nature, or Under-Burden-Failing group, *Julius Cæsar, Hamlet, Meas. for Meas.*; *b.* the Tempter-Yielding group, *Othello, Macbeth* ; *c.* the first Ingratitude and Cursing Play, *Lear* ; *d.* the Lust or False-Love group, *Troilus, Antony & Cleopatra* ; *e.* the second Ingratitude and Cursing group, *Coriolanus, Timon.*

And thus, forgiven and forgiving,[1] full of the highest wisdom and of peace, at one with family, and friends, and foes, in harmony with Avon's flow and Stratford's level meads, Shakspere closd his life on earth.[2]

[1] It is certain, I think, that in his latest plays, of the Fourth Period, Shakspere was also teaching himself the lesson of forgiveness for the wrongs and disappointments he had sufferd, and which were reflected in the Tragedies of his Third Period. See on this my friend Prof. Dowden's forthcoming 'Mind and Art of Shakspere' (H. S. King & Co.), with its fine and right likening of Shakspere to a ship, beaten and storm-tost, but yet entering harbour with sails full-set, to anchor in peace. I quote it from the MS. of his Lectures:—

'There are lovers of Shakspere so jealous of his honour that they are unable to suppose that any grave moral flaw could have impaired the perfection of his life and manhood. To me Shakspere appears to have been a man who, by strenuous effort and with the aid of the good powers of the world, saved himself,—so as by fire. Before Shakspere zealots demand our attention to ingenious theories to establish the immaculateness of Shakspere's life, let them show that his writings never offend. When they have shown that Shakspere's poetry possesses the proud virginity of Milton's poetry, they may then go on to show that Shakspere's youth was devoted to an ideal of moral purity and elevation like the youth of Milton. I certainly should not infer from Shakspere's writings that he held himself with virginal strength and pride remote from the blameful pleasures of the world. What I do *not* find anywhere in the plays of Shakspere is a single cold-blooded, hard or selfish line—all is warm, sensitive, vital, radiant with delight, or a-thrill with pain. And what I dare to affirm of Shakspere's life is, that whatever its sins may have been, they were not hard, selfish, deliberate, cold-blooded sins. The errors of his heart originated in his sensitiveness, in his imagination (not at first strictly trained to fidelity to the fact), in his quick sense of existence, and in the self-abandoning devotion of his heart. There are some noble lines by Chapman in which he pictures to himself the life of great energy, enthusiasms and passions, which for ever stands upon the edge of utmost danger, and yet for ever remains in absolute security:—

> Give me a spirit that on life's rough sea
> Loves to have his sails filled with a lusty wind
> Even till his sail-yards tremble, his masts crack,
> And his rapt ship runs on her side so low
> That she drinks water, and her keel ploughs air;
> There is no danger to the man that knows
> What life and death is; there's not any law
> Exceeds his knowledge; neither is it lawful
> That he should stoop to any other law.

Such a master-spirit pressing forward under strained canvas was Shakspere. If the ship dipped and drank water, she rose again; and at length we see her within view of her haven, sailing under a large, calm wind, not without tokens of stress of weather, but if battered, yet unbroken, by the waves. It is to dull lethargic lives that a moral accident is fatal, because they are tending no whither, and lack energy and momentum to right themselves again. To say anything against decent lethargic vices and timid virtues, anything to the advantage of the strenuous life of bold action and eager emotion which necessarily incurs risks and sometimes suffers, is, I am aware, "dangerous." Well, then, be it so; it is dangerous.'

[2] In his *History of New Place*, Mr. Halliwell has suggested a more probable cause for Shakspere's death than the no doubt groundless traditional one (after 1662) of the drinking bout with Drayton and Ben Jonson, namely, that the

Now all that I have written on the succession of Shakspere's works in relation to the man Shakspere is liable to the objector's ' Pooh ! all stuff ! Shakspere wrote comedies and tragedies for his company just as the Burbages told him to. His comedies were produc'd for some leading comic actor, and his tragedies for his friend and partner Richard Burbage, the great tragedian. Neither reflected his own feelings, except professionally, any more than Macbeth's or Othello's did Burbage's when he acted them.' Take it so, if you will ; but still, I say, Do follow the course of Shakspere's mind ; still do commune with the creations of his brain as they flowd from it ; still note his wondrous growth in that sensibility and intensity, far beyond all other men's, that enabld him to throw himself into all the varid figures of his plays with ever-increasing power and skill ; still watch his greatening of wisdom and knowledge of life, his dazzling wit and ever-flowing humour ; still gaze at, and glory in, his dream of, nay, his breathing and living Fair Women, who enchant even Taine, and win the reverence of Gervinus and all true-sould men—beside whom Dante's Beatrice alone is fit to stand :—and then ask yourself whether the choice of Shakspere's series of subjects was fixt by others' orders, or chance, *or* by his own frame of mind, his own mood ; whether his young plays of love and fun, of patriotism and war,[1] of humour and wit, showd his own early manhood or not, his time of successful struggle, and happy enjoyment of its fruits ; whether the dark questionings of ' Hamlet,' the mingling with lawlessness, treachery, hatred, revenge, had nothing to do with his own later inner life, with that ' *hell of time* ' which he tells us he passt through during his quarrel with his friend [2] ; whether the reconciliation and peace of his latest plays were independent of his new quiet home-life at Stratford with its peace. I am content to abide by your answer. Depend on it that what our greatest Victorian poetess, Mrs. Barrett Browning, though a lyrist, said of her own poetry, is true, to a great extent, of Shakspere in his dramas, ' They have my heart and life in them ; they are not empty shells.' The feelings were in his soul ; he put them into words ; and that is why the world is at his feet.

pigsties and nuisances which the Corporation books show to have existed in Chapel Lane, which ran the whole length of New Place, bred the fever of which Shakspere is said to have died.

Mr. Halliwell gives several extracts from the books, as ' 1605 : the Chamberlaines shall gyve warning to Henry Smyth to plucke downe his pigges cote which is built nere the chapple wall, and the house of office (= privy) there.'—*New Place*, p. 29.

[1] They had, and naturally, their leaven of pathos and tragedy, as I have shown above.

[2]
> For if you were by my unkindness shaken,
> As I by yours, you have passt *a hell of time.*
> Sonnet 120, l. 6.

TRIAL TABLE OF THE ORDER OF SHAKSPERE'S PLAYS.

[This, like all other tables, must be lookt on as merely tentative, and open to modification for any good reasons. But if only it comes near the truth, then reading the plays in its order will the sooner enable the student to find out its mistakes. (M. stands for 'mentioned by Francis Meres in his *Palladis Tamia*, 1598.') In his introductory Essays to *Shakespeare's Dramatische Werke* (German Shakespeare Society) Prof. Hertzberg dates *Titus* 1587–9, *Love's Labours Lost* 1592, *Comedy of Errors* about New Year's Day 1591, *Two Gentlemen* 1592, *All's Well* 1603, *Troilus and Cressida* 1603, and *Cymbeline* 1611. Mr. Grant White dates *Richard II.* 1595, *Richard III.* 1593–4.]

	Suppos'd Date	Earliest Allusion	Date of Publication
FIRST PERIOD.			
Titus Andronicus toucht up . .	(?) 1588	1594 M	[(?) 1594] 1600
Love's Labours Lost . . .	1588–9	1598 M	1598 (amended)
[Loves Labours Wonne . . .	]	1598 M	
Comedy of Errors	1589–91	1594 M	1623
Midsummer Night's Dream (? 2 dates)	1590–1	1598 M	1600
Two Gentlemen of Verona . .	1590–2	1598 M	1623
(?) 1 Henry VI. toucht up . .	(?) 1590–2		1623
Romeo and Juliet	1591–3	1595 M	1597
Venus and Adonis	1592–3		1593
Lucrece	1593–4	1594	1594
(?) A Lover's Complaint (? not Shakspere's). . . .			
Richard II.	(?) 1593–4	? 1595 M	1597
2 & 3 Henry VI. recast . . .	(?) 1592–4		1623
Richard III.	1594	? 1595 M	1597
SECOND PERIOD.			
John	1595	1598 M	1623
Merchant of Venice . . .	1596	1598 M	1600†
Taming of the Shrew, part . .	(?) 1596–7		1623 ¹
1 Henry IV.	1596–7‡	1598 M	1598
2 Henry IV.	1597–8‡	1598 M	1600
Merry Wives	1598–9	1602	1602
Henry V.	1599‡	1599	1600
Much Ado	1599–1600‡	1600	1600
As you Like it	1600‡	1600	1623§
Twelfth Night	1601‡	1602	1623
All's Well (? L.'s L. Wonne recast).	1601–2		1623
Sonnets	(?) 1592–1608	1598 M	1609
THIRD PERIOD.			
Julius Cæsar	1601	1601	1623
Hamlet	1602–3‡	(?)	1603*
Measure for Measure . . .	(?) 1603		1623
Othello	(?) 1604	1610	1622

* Enter'd 1 year before at Stationers' Hall.
† Enter'd 2 years before at Stationers' Hall.
‡ May be lookt-on as fairly certain.
§ Enter'd in the Stationers' Registers in 1600.
¹ 'The Taming of *a* Shrew' was publisht in 1604.

Trial Table of the Order of Shakspere's Plays—continu'd.

	Supposd Date	Earliest Allusion	Date of Publication
Macbeth	1605–6‡	1610	1623
Lear	1605–6‡	1606	1608*
Troilus and Cressida . . .	(?) 1606–7	1609	1609
Antony and Cleopatra . . .	1606–7	1608 (?)	1623
Coriolanus	(?) 1607–8		1623
Timon, part	1607–8		1623
FOURTH PERIOD.			
Pericles, part	1608‡	1608	1609*
Tempest	(?) 1610	?1614	1623
Cymbeline	1610–12		1623
Winter's Tale	(?) 1611	1611	1623
Two Noble Kinsmen, part . .	(?) 1612		1634
Henry VIII., part	1613‡	1613 (?)	1623

* Enterd 1 year before at Stationers' Hall.
‡ May be lookt-on as fairly certain.

§ 6. Now of a few helps to reading Shakspere. 1. As to Text : have the ' Globe ' edition (Macmillan, 3s. 6d.) because its lines are numberd, and for sound text ; but do not ruin your eyes by reading it. For reading, get a small 8vo. clear-type edition like Singer's, with notes —a cheap re-issue, in half-crown volumes, is just coming out (G. Bell and Sons). Get (if you can afford it) Mr. Furness's admirable Variorum edition of *Romeo and Juliet* and *Macbeth* (15s. each, A. R. Smith) ; *Hamlet* is preparing ; (the other plays will slowly follow") ; and, for their notes, Messrs. Clark and Wright's little Clarendon-Press edition of plays at 1s. or 1s. 6d. each (their 8vo. Cambridge edition with most valuable full collations, is out of print) ; and Craik's *Julius Cæsar*. 2. Glossaries, &c. : Mrs. Cowden Clarke's ' Concordance ' to the Plays (25s.), and Mrs. H. H. Furness's to the Minor Poems (15s.) ; Dr. Schmidt's most useful 'Shakespeare-Lexicon' (vol. i., A to L, 13s. 6d. Williams and Norgate), which well arranges the passages under their senses, and the parts of speech of the head-word ; Dyce's ' Glossary ' (last vol. of his Shakspere), and Nares's 'Glossary' (2 vols., 24s., A. R. Smith). 3. Grammar and Metre : Dr. Abbott's ' Shakespearian Grammar ' (Macmillan, 6s.) indispensable ; but with some misscansions that will ' absolutely scar ' you, as Mr. Ellis says, and over some of which you will groan, as we did in concert at the Philological Society when Professor Mayor read them (see his Paper in ' Phil. Soc. Trans.,' 1874, now in the press. Dr. Abbott, I need not say, ridicules our scannings). W. Sidney Walker's three volumes of Shakspere Text-criticism (15s., A. R. Smith) are excellent.[1] C. Bathurst's capital little half-crown volume

_____
[1] Dr. Ingleby describes his just publisht *Still Lion* as ' indications of a

on the end-stopt and unstopt line,—' Changes in Shakespeare's Versification at different Periods of his Life ' (J. W. Parker and Son)
—is unluckily out of print. 4. Pronunciation: Mr. A. J. Ellis's
' Early English Pronunciation with Special Reference to Chaucer
and Shakespeare ' (three Parts, 30s., Asher and Co.; or Part iii.
only, the Shakespeare Part [p. 917–96], 10s.). 5. Commentaries:
Gervinus's (14s., Smith, Elder & Co.)[1]; Mrs. Jameson's ' Characteristics of Women,' that is, Shakspere's Women—an enthusiastic and
beautiful book (5s., Routledge); Prof. Dowden's excellent ' Mind
and Art of Shakspere ' (12s., H. S. King and Co.); S. T. Coleridge's
' Shakespeare Lectures,' &c. (3s. 6d., Howell); Watkiss Lloyd's
' Critical Essays on the Plays ' (2s. 6d., Bell); my Introduction to the
' Leopold Shakspere ' (Cassell & Co., 10s. 6d.); T. P. Courtenay's
matter-of-fact ' Commentaries on the Historical Plays ' (2 vols., Colburn,
1840). Then, if you can afford more books, buy Hudson's ' Shakespeare, his Life, Art, and Characters ' (of his twenty-five greatest
plays) (2 vols., 12s., Sampson Low); ' Ulrici' (7s., Bell); Schlegel's
' Dramatic Art' (3s. 6d.), and Hazlitt's thin ' Characters of Shakespeare's Plays ' (2s., G. Bell and Sons); Mr. John R. Wise's charming
little book on ' Shakespeare; his Birthplace and its Neighbourhood'
(3s. 6d., Smith, Elder and Co.); Mr. Roach Smith's ' Rural Life of
Shakespeare ' (3s. 6d., George Bell and Sons). Buy a copy of Booth's
admirable Reprint of the First Folio of 1623 (12s. 6d., Glaisher, 265,
High Holborn; with the Quarto of ' Much Adoe,' for 1s.). For the
facts of Shakspere's Life, chronologically arrangd, Mr. S. Neil's ' Shakespeare: a Critical Biography ' (Houlston and Wright, 1s. 6d.) is a
fair book. On the ' Sonnets,' get the best book, Armitage Brown's
(? 6s., A. R. Smith); for the allegorical view of them, the late Mr. R.
Simpson's ' Philosophy of Shakespeare's Sonnets ' (3s. 6d., Trübner).
—Of course, subscribe a guinea a year to the New Shakspere Society
(Hon. Sec., A. G. Snelgrove, Esq., London Hospital, E), read its
Papers, and work its Texts, specially the parallel ones.

Get one or two likely friends to join you in your Shakspere work,
if you can, and fight out all your and their difficulties in common:
worry every line; eschew the vice of wholesale emendation. Get up
a party of ten or twelve men and four or six women to read the plays
in succession at one another's houses, or elsewhere. once a fortnight,
and discuss each for half an hour after each reading. Do all you can
to further the study of Shakspere, chronologically and as a whole,
throughout the nation.

systematic Hermeneutic [science of interpretation] of Shakspere's text.' It is
strongly against plausible emendations, and is well worth careful study.

[1] Prof. Dowden, who has been through all the German commentators, thinks
Kreyssig's *Vorlesungen über Shakespeare* (a big book), and *Shakespeare-Fragen*
(a little book), the best popular introduction in German to Shakspere.

Lastly, go to Stratford-upon-Avon, and see the town where Shakspere was born, and bred, and died; the country over which he wanderd and playd when a boy, whose beauties and whose lore, as a man, he put into his plays. Go either in spring, in April, 'when the greatest poet was born in Nature's sweetest time,' and let Mr. Wise ('Shakespeare: his Birthplace and its Neighbourhood,' p. 44, 58, &c.) tell you how 'everything is full of beauty' that you'll see; or go in full summer, as I did one afternoon in July this year. See first the little low room where tradition says Shakspere was born, though his father did not buy the house till eleven years after his birth;[1] look at the foundations of 'New Place,' walk on the site of Shakspere's house, in the garden whose soil he must often have trod, thinking of his boyhood and hasty marriage, of London, with its trials and triumphs, and the wonders he had created for its delight; follow his body, past the school where he learnt, to its grave in the Avon-side church ringd with elms; see the worn slab that covers his bones, with wife's and daughter's beside; look up at the bust which figures the case of the brain and heart that have so enricht the world, which shows you more truly than anything else what Shakspere was like in the flesh; try to see in those hazel eyes, those death-drawn lips,[2] those ruddy cheeks, the light, the merriment, the tenderness, the wisdom, and love that once were theirs; walk by the full and quiet Avon's side, where the swan sails gently, by which the cattle feed; ask yourself what word sums up your feelings on these scenes: and answer, with me, 'Peace'!

Next morning, walk up the Welcombe road, across the old common lands whose enclosing Shakspere said 'he was not able to bear:' when up Rowley Bank, turn round; see the town nestle under its circling hills, shut in on the left by its green wall of trees. The corn is golden beside you. Meon Hill meets the sky in your front; its shoulder slants sharply to the spire of the church where Shakespeare's dust lies: away on the right is Broadway, lit with the sun; below it the ridge of

[1] He *may* have rented it before; but I expect that the former house, in Henley Street, in which John Shakspere dwelt, would have a better claim to be 'the birthplace,' if it were now known.

[2] 'We may mention—on the authority of Mr. Butcher, the very courteous clerk of Stratford Church, who saw the examination made—that two years ago Mr. Story, the great American sculptor, when at Stratford, made a very careful examination of Shakspere's bust from a raised scaffolding, and came to the conclusion that the face of the bust was modelled from a death-mask. The lower part of the face was very death-like; the upper lip was elongated and drawn up from the lower one by the shrinking of the nostrils, the first part of the face to 'go' after death; the eyebrows were neither of the same length nor on the same level; the depth from the eye to the ear was extraordinary; the cheeks were of different shapes, the left one being the more prominent at top. On the whole, Mr. Story felt certain of the bust being made from a death-mask.'—F. J. F., in *The Academy,* Aug. 22, 1874, p. 205, col. 3. *The Academy,* our 'leading literary paper,' should be read for Shakspere news.

Roomer Hill, yellow for harvest on the right, passing leftwards into a
dark belt of trees to the church, their hollows filled with blue haze. In
this nest is Shakspere's town. After gazing your fill on the fair
scene before you, walk to the boat-place, paddle out for the best view
of the elm-fram̃d church, then by its river-borderd side to the stream
below; get a beautiful view of the tower through a vista of trees
beyond the low waterfall; then pass by cattle half-knee deep in the
shallows, sluggishly whisking their tails, happily chewing the cud; go
under Wire-Brake bank, whose trees droop down to the river, whose
wood-pigeons greet you with coos; past many groups of grey willows,
with showers of wild roses between; feathery reeds rise beside you,
birds twitter about, the sky is blue overhead, your boat glides smoothly
down stream: you feel the sweet content with which Shakspere must have
lookt on the scene. Later, you wander to Shottery, to Ann Hathaway's
cottage, where perchance in hot youth the poet made love. Then you ride
through Charlecote's tall-elmd park, and see the deer whose ancestors
he may have stolen; on to Warwick, with its castle rising grandly from
Avon bank; back to Stratford, with a glorious view from the hill, on
your left in your homeward ride.[1] Evening comes: you stroll again
by the riverside, through groups of townsfolk pleasant to see, in well-to-
do Sunday dress. From Cross-o'-th'-Hill you look at the fine view of
church and town, backt by the Welcombe Hills; through Wire Brake [2]
and ripe corn, you walk to the bridge that brings you to the opposite
level bank of the stream. Then you lie down, chatting of Shakspere
to your friend, while lovers in pairs pass lingering by, and the twilight
comes. Then again you say that the peace of the place was fit for
Shakspere's end, and that the memory of its quiet beauty will never
away from your mind.

Yes, Stratford will help you to understand Shakspere.

———

These pages aim at giving, shortly, to beginners, such parts of the
result of my last year's work at Shakspere—in scanty leisure—as I
wish some one had given me on my first start at him. Of their im-
maturity, beside the ripeness of Gervinus, and of their unworthiness
to appear before his book, I am only too painfully conscious. But as I
have gone among working-men and private friends, I have been askt
to put some of these things in print; and for my haste in thus doing it
I willingly risk the blame of those who know far more than I do, being

---

[1] If you can, get on to ruind Kenilworth, where Shakspere may have seen
Leicester's pageants before Elizabeth, in 1575 (see my edition of *Captain Cox,*
Ballad Society), to use in *Midsummer Night's Dream.* Heaven forbid that he
should have turnd the great mason Captain into Bottom !

[2] The young Stratford folk call their Sunday-evening stroll through this
woodod bank, ' Going to Chapel.' That their devotions interested the attendants,
I can say.

d

assurd that what I have written will be of use to others who know somewhat less than myself. Work at Shakspere, serious intelligent work, is what I want, from thousands of men and women who have hitherto neglected him. If they will give me that, they may abuse as they like, the mistakes they may find in these hints.

My thanks are due to my friends Professors Hertzberg, Wagner, Seeley, and Dowden, Mr. Spedding, Mr. Hales, Dr. Abbott, Mr. Halliwell, Dr. Ingleby, Mr. Aldis Wright, Mr. Wheatley, Mr. Malleson, &c. for their hints on this Introduction.

F. J. FURNIVALL.

3 St. George's Square, N.W.
Sept. 16, 1874, *and*
April 8, 1877.

P.S.—Prof. Ingram, of Trin. Coll., Dublin, has just (Nov. 8) sent me his Paper on the weak- and light-endings in Shakspere. The 16 *weak-endings* are ' and, but (=L. *sed,* and=*except*), by, for, from, if[1], on, nor, or, than, that, to, with.' The 54 *light-endings* are ' am, are, art, be, been, but (=only), can, could, did[2], do[2], does[2], dost[2], ere, had[2], has[2], hast[2], have[2], he, how[3], I, into, is, like, may, might, shall, shalt, she, should, since, so[4], such[4], they, thou, though, through, till, upon, was, we, were, what[5], when[5], where[5], which, while, whilst, who[5], whom[5], why[5], will, would, yet (=*tamen*), you.' Here is an extract from his

[1] Except in the combination *as if.*

[2] Only when us'd as auxiliaries.

[3] When not directly interrogative.

[4] When followd immediately by *as. Such* also, when followd by a substantive with an indefinite article, as 'Such a man.'

[5] When not directly interrogative. Prof. Ingram's Paper will appear in *The New Shakspere Society's Transactions,* Part 2. He says :—

'The weak-endings do not come in by slow degrees, but the poet seems to have thrown himself at once into this new structure of verse ; 28 examples occurring in *Antony and Cleopatra,* whilst there are not more than two in any earlier play. . . .

'As long as the light-endings remain very few, no conclusion with respect to the order of the plays can be based on them.

'But the very marked increase of their number in *Macbeth,* showing a strong development of the same tendency which, further on, produced the large number of weak-endings, seems to show that it was the latest of the plays preceding the weak-ending period. . . .

'An examination of the weak-endings in *Henry VIII.* strikingly confirms the conclusions of Mr. Spedding respecting the two different systems of verse which co-exist in that play. In the Shaksperian portion, as marked off by him, there are 45 light-endings against 6 in Fletcher's part, and 37 weak-endings against 1 in Fletcher's part. And these weak-endings occur in every Shaksperian scene. The one weak-ending in Fletcher's portion occurs in a scene (iv. 1) which has not been uniformly assigned to Fletcher, and which, it is curious to observe, of all the Shaksperian scenes in the play approaches, in the matter of the feminine ending, nearest to Fletcher. . . . The date, also, which has been assigned by Mr. Spedding

table of these endings in the late plays, whose order alone they help to settle :—

	No. of light endings	No. of weak endings	No. of Verse lines in play	Percentage of light endings	Percentage of weak endings	Percentage of both together
Macbeth	21	2				
Timon '	15	?	1112	1·35	?	?
Antony and Cleopatra .	71	28	2803	2·53	1·00	3·53
Coriolanus	60	44	2563	2·34	1·71	4·05
Pericles (Shakspere part)	20	10	719	2·78	1·39	4·17
Tempest	42	25	1460	2·88	1·71	4·59
Cymbeline	78	52	2692	2·90	1·93	4·83
Winter's Tale	57	45	1825	3·12	2·47	5·59
Two Noble Kinsmen (non-Fletcher part) .	50	34	1378	3·63	2·47	6·10
Henry VIII. (Sh's. part)	45	37	1146	3·93	3·23	7·16

to Shakspere's portion of *Henry VIII.* is confirmed by the Table, in opposition to the views of Elze and others. It appears to be without doubt his latest work ; a conclusion which quite falls in with what is known from an external source as to the production in 1613 of a play which there is every reason to believe was the same.

'With respect to *The Two Noble Kinsmen,* the weak-ending test confirms what has been otherwise shown by Mr. Hickson and others, namely, that here again there are two different systems of verse. In Fletcher's part there are 3 light endings to 50 in the other portion, and 1 weak-ending to 34. The weak-endings are found in every non-Fletcherian scene but two. One is i. 4, in which there are, exclusive of a song, but six lines in all. The other is iii. 3, which, curiously enough, as Mr. Furnivall remarks, the stopt-line test would give to Fletcher. The scene is one about which, notwithstanding what has been said by Mr. Hickson, there is not much to mark the authorship.

'The answer to the question—Who was the author of the non-Fletcherian portion of this play ?—does not force itself on my mind with the same clear evidence as the conviction that the non-Shaksperian part of *Henry VIII* is by Fletcher. The choice of the story, in which the passion is, after all, of an artificial kind, the toleration of the "trash" which abounds in the underplot, the faintness (as I must persist in calling it) of the characterization, and, in general, the absence, except in occasional flashes, of the splendid genius which shows itself all through the last period of Shakspere, I have always found very perplexing. In reading the (so-called) Shaksperian part of the play, I do not often feel myself in contact with a mind of the first order. Still, it is certain that there is much in it that is *like* Shakspere, and some things that are worthy of him at his best ; that the manner, in general, is more that of Shakspere than of any other contemporary dramatist ; and that the system of verse is one which we do not find in any other, whilst it is, in all essentials, that of Shakspere's last period. I cannot name any one else who could have written this portion of the play. The weak-ending affords a ready test of the correctness of Knight's notion that Chapman was the writer. I have examined the play of *Bussy d'Ambois,* and do not find in it a single instance of the weak-ending, and, turning rapidly over Chapman's whole works, I see no evidence that he was ever at all given to it. If Shakspere be—as we seem forced to believe—the author of the part of *The Two Noble Kinsmen* now usually attributed to him, this will take its place in the series of his works between the *Winter's Tale* and *Henry VIII.*'

ADDRESS

TO THE

NEW SHAKSPERE SOCIETY

OF LONDON.

— •••—

DISCOVERY

OF

LORD VERULAM'S UNDOUBTED AUTHORSHIP

OF THE

"SHAKSPERE" WORKS.

BY

MRS C. F. ASHMEAD WINDLE.

SAN FRANCISCO:
JOSEPH WINTERBURN & Co., BOOK AND JOB PRINTERS AND ELECTROTYPERS.
1881.

Gentlemen of the New Shakspere Society of London :

I have the honor of informing your distinguished Association that I have discovered an allegorical under-meaning, running throughout the works called "Shakespeare's," disclosing their author to have been undoubtedly your distinguished countryman, FRANCIS BACON, LORD VERULAM—already, before this halo to illumine his honors, the proudest name on the roll of English fame.

It is about two years and a half since—entirely of myself—I made the discovery to which I have alluded, and, my life being very retired, I have had no opportunity of communicating with any one versed in these dramas, with a view to making it generally known. Feeling more and more deeply that my revelation is of imperative importance to the memory of the illustrious Bacon, to the English nation, and to the whole literary world, I have now determined to communicate directly with your Society in regard to its public announcement, as, my health being lately delicate, I am liable to quit the world at any time, leaving it unrevealed.

To satisfy you that my overture of a discovery so momentous is nothing chimerical or unsustained, I submit respectfully to you herewith my under-reading of the play of "CYMBELINE."

CYMBELINE.

———•-•———

The play of CYMBELINE has universally been a favorite among the
so-called Shakespeare dramas, and, out of much study, both of the
closet and of the stage, has not unfrequently borne the palm of greatest praise among the glorious galaxy to which it belongs. Mr. Swinburne, in his recent "Study of Shakespeare," calls it "the play of
plays," lovingly reserving for it the finishing touches of his eloquent
handling of the theme from a former standpoint.

But, people of England—the land which gave the world the one
unequalled fame of these matchless dramas—and you, gentlemen of
the New Shakspere Society of London—the city whose ground is made
sacred by the once bodily foot-prints of the one earthly demigod, whose
like the world never saw before, nor ever will see again, in the writer
of these plays—I have a new presentation of CYMBELINE, to which I
respectfully invite your particular, honorable and reverent attention.

I propose to show you that the author, too, has given to this particular drama so much of his own favoritism as to have committed to
it the definite statement of THE ENIGMA he had left to posterity in the
volume of his dramas. Briefly to preface, I propose to show you this
play as a VEILED ALLEGORY, placed by the author at the end of his book
as *the appropriate termination of a series of similar allegories, or semi-
allegories, bearing throughout the burden of the same* ENIGMA—thus confidently to commit, as well as distinctly to suggest, its propounded
SECRET to the chances of futurity. I shall disclose to you the great
author here pathetically and divinely, in the form of this most touching
and exquisite allegory, renouncing the fame of his dramas, as for himself personally, in his own day and generation, lest this should extin-
guish them for posterity; but yet in the end predicting, with an assurance of Jovian prophecy, that this severed branch of his fame shoulds
with those other "lopped" branches of his philosophy and virtuou,
character, in coming time be restored to his name in the spreading
honors of his beloved England.

I should premise that the KEY to the running allegory involved in
the dramas is contained in the *mystery of the sonnets*. This mystery
once pierced, and carried into the reading of the plays, reveals *an absolute divineness of ideality underlying their mere outward form, as well as*

4

a plaintive autobiographical information of the poet's consciousness, enhancing them above all possible eulogy, save that tacit one of reciprocal apprehension of miracle performed. I infer, from this necessary relation of the sonnets to the plays, that it was for such reason, when CYMBELINE was produced from the author's pen, in 1609, with its final definite proposition of his continuous ENIGMA, that the *sonnets* were in the same year issued from the press. He no doubt must then have expected that this would be the last play he should write. It is a circumstance perhaps not undeserving of notice in this connection, that after that date *William Shakespeare* returned no more to London from the oblivion of Stratford.

Suitably to the evident design of CYMBELINE, whatever other plays may, through change of plan, have been produced after it in the order of time, it still takes its intended and fitting place at the end of the folio of 1623, presenting the GREAT VOLUME'S ENIGMA at its close.

I have found that all the names of the *dramatis personæ* are *symbolical*, being severally significant in the vital allegory concealed under their outward manifestation. Interwoven with a tale of Boccacio's, a portion of "Holinshed's Chronicles," and an original episode, the author has—in seemingly fictitious personifications merely, and under the designation of comedy—written the crowning tragedy of a life, out of which (on account of his transcending sensibilities, want of appreciation and the force of adverse circumstances) all the overpowering tragedy in his works became expressed. Hence, for the purpose of rendering to you the allegory, it is requisite that I should give you, before entering upon it, the following

KEY TO CYMBELINE.

EXPLANATION OF THE SYMBOLICAL NAMES OF PERSONAGES.

CYMBELINE : A cymbal[*]. (Used here to represent Britain in the *expansion* of her Fame; that is, in the following sense : "'Tiberius Cæsar *cymbalum mundi* vocabat" —*filled the world* with his discussions. *Pliny* and *Virgil*.)

LEONATUS POSTHUMUS: (British) Lion-born Posthumously.

CLOTEN: Clothing. (Intending the living bodily personality, as but the *clothing* of the immortal parts, transmitted in knowledge and character.)

BELARIUS: Bel-Air, or Fine Air. (Referring to the lofty atmosphere of study and thought.)
(Otherwise called)

MORGAN: My Organ (Meaning the " Novum *Organum*.")

---

[*] NOTE.—Bacon, in his essay on "Judicature," used the *cymbal* as a figure to express the award of just sentence, as, "An over-speaking judge is no well-tuned *cymbal*."

GUIDERIUS: As a Guide.

(Otherwise called) — The Learned Philosopher.

POLYDORE: Many Ores.

ARVIRAGUS: As with the Art of Manhood.

(Otherwise called) — The Virtuous Man.

CADWAL: Strong and harmonious, through self-government.

QUEEN; Second Wife to Cymbeline: The existing day or generation of British Fame.

IMOGEN: Image-in. (Imagination depicted.)

IACHIMO; Slander.

PISANIO: Fear.

SICILIUS: ~~Sonnet~~ The GENIUS invoked in the *Sonnets* *—(a form of poem of SICILIAN origin, and introduced by Dante into Italy.

TENANTIUS: Dweller in the *Sonnets*.

EURIPHILE: Lover of Discovery.

The foregoing explanation will not, however, be complete until I shall connect each of the symbolical characters with the ONE MAN to whom in the allegory they are all meant to apply—most of them, indeed, representing only himself in some one or other of his divers characteristics. This Protean individual, who should he be? None other than the Protean English demigod who has written his own name in them in his ENIGMA—as will appear when I shall have unfolded it to his breathless countrymen as FRANCIS of VERULAM; and Englishmen, and gentlemen of the New Shakespeare Society! I pray you bend your heads to its sacred memory, as it is read, for it wears the halo of the cross above its crown.

CYMBELINE as King of Britain, *represents Great Britain and her national Fame.* The play opens in a garden behind the palace. Two gentlemen of the Court are conversing upon the changed aspect of the faces of the nobles and courtiers since his daughter's recent marriage to POSTHUMUS, against the will of her father, who has designed her for the son of his second wife. This brings about a description by one of them of POSTHUMUS, who *symbolizes the posthumous fame of Bacon;* for, although the speaker could "not delve him to the root," it was stated that he was the son of SICILIUS, who "had his titles by TENANTIUS." Now the sonnet form of poetry was of SICILIAN origin. SICILIUS, therefore, signifies the poetic GENIUS invoked in the sonnets of this author, as a "lovely boy," and besought to beget "copies" of itself which should gain an endur-

---

* NOTE.—The writer, in the *Sonnets* invoked his genius to wed, and to beget heirs for *posterity.* Hence "Posthumus," or fame after death.

ing fame in posterity. Hence POSTHUMUS, in being the son of SICILIUS, is designed to represent this future fame promised in the SONNETS. TENANTIUS, by whom SICILIUS "had his titles" of beauty, grace and honour beyond all comparison, *was the writer or dweller in the Sonnets* who, for his patriotic services "gained the sur-addition, LEONATUS;" and he, of course, signifies, the author of the dramas, Francis Bacon. Posthumus is thus described by the conversation:

" *1st Gent.* A creature such
As to seek through the regions of the earth
For one his like, there would be something falling
In him that should compare. I do not think
So fair an outward, and such stuff within
Endows a man but he.

2nd Gent. You *speak him far.*

1st Gent. I do extend him, sir, within himself;
Crush him together, rather than unfold
His measure duly."

Such was the great author's conscious measurement of his future proper recognition, told in allegory; but he knew it would not be until distant time, and that to speak thus of himself in the play was to "speak him far." What a meaning do not these three monosyllables take on in this new light!

Then one of the speakers relates how the father of Posthumus had died of a broken heart caused by the death of "two LEONATI, his sons "—*offspring of the same Genius which created Posthumus*, and *meaning the poems of* "*Venus and Adonis," and "Tarquin and Lucrece,*" not included in the folio, and hence presumed by the author to be lost to his future fame. The narrator goes on to tell how Posthumus was born after his father's death, adopted by the king, and named Posthumus Leonatus; and thus describes his breeding and training at the Court—presenting, under the allegory, a beautiful picture of Bacon's own childhood.

" *1st Gent.* The king, he takes the babe
To his protection, calls him Posthumus Leonatus;
Breeds him, and makes him of his bed-chamber;
Puts him to all the learnings that his time
Could make him the receiver of; which he took
As we do air, fast as 'twas ministered; and
In his spring became a harvest: Lived in Court
(Which rare it is to do) most praised, most loved,
A sample to the youngest; to the more mature
A glass that feated them; and to the graver
A child that guided dotards."

This praise of Posthumus is crowned by the assertion that the preference of Imogen for Posthumus, and her marrying him against her father's will was sufficient to show his quality:

" *1st Gent.* Her own price
Proclaims how she esteemed him and his virtue ;
By her election may be truly read
What kind of man he is."

Now IMOGEN, from the Latin *Imo* (the opposite to what appears) *signifies the Image-in, or imagination of Bacon, as depicted in the dramas.* The QUEEN, her step-mother, *second wife to Cymbeline, represents the age or period of British history in which Bacon lived.* Cymbeline, the king, or Britain, wishes to marry Imogen (the dramas) to the Queen's son Cloten. CLOTEN, from Clotho (the spinner of individual fate) is the *clothing* of Bacon, *meaning Bacon's mere living personality,* which, *as the Queen's son, was the product of his time and circumstances,* but which was only the outward garb of the true Man, the Philosopher, and the Poet it enveloped as a garment.

After the marriage of Posthumus and Imogen contrary to the wish of Cymbeline, the king orders him away from the Court and Britain. This leads me to explain that *the separation of Posthumus from Imogen is designed to figure Bacon's separation of his fame from the plays until futurity.*

The Queen, in Act 1, Scene 2d, attempts to offer consolation to Imogen and Posthumus, in the prospect of their parting:

> "*Queen.*   No, be assured, you shall not find me, daughter,
> After the slander of most step-mothers,
> Evil-eyed unto you: you are my prisoner,
> But *my gaoler shall deliver you the keys*
> *That lock up your restraint.*"

This signifies that the circumstances of the moment did not permit Bacon to claim the plays, but that *they should nevertheless have the freedom of the public.*

The Queen then says to Posthumus:

> "*Queen.*   For you, Posthumus,
> So soon as I can win the offended king
> I will be known your advocate: *marry, yet,*
> *The fire of rage is in him*; and *'twere good*
> *You leaned unto his sentence with what patience*
> *Your wisdom may inform you.*"

The "marry" in the foregoing is not, in the under-sense, an interjection only, as it seems in the outward construction, but it means that it will not do yet for Bacon to *marry his name to his dramas,* during some occasion of national offence connected with them, and therefore, it were the part of "wisdom" to bear his "sentence" with what "patience" he could. The Queen's seeming encouragement to them against her real objections, indicates the delusive hopes the author at first entertained, of being able to acknowledge his works in his own day. The Queen, having left Posthumus and Imogen alone, Imogen says, with a fine touch, in the allegory, of Bacon's suffrance as a

---

* *Note.* For through the painter must you see his skill
To find where your true *image pictured* lies.—Sonnet 24.

courtier, and showing an instance of his committing the record of such suffering to the pages of the dramas:

> "*Imogen.* O dissembling courtesy! How fine this tyrant
> Can tickle when she wounds!"

and then Imogen proceeds, with assurance of her capacity of endurance under adverse conditions, in the hope of their re-union—meaning the assured endurance of Bacon's future fame in the dramas:

> "*Imogen.* My dearest husband,
> I something fear my father's wrath, but nothing
> (Always reserved my holy duty), what
> His rage can do on me : *You must be gone;*
> *And I shall here abide the shot*
> *Of angry eyes; not comforted to live*
> *But that there is this jewel in the world*
> *That I may see again."*

Then Posthumus utters his regrets to leave her:

> "*Post.* My Queen! my mistress!
> *O lady weep no more! lest I give cause*
> *To be suspected of more tenderness*
> *Than doth become a man!*

As much as for Bacon to say : "O my dramas! *let me not show too much grief in your pages* for this our separation of name, lest the world should realize the pathos of that necessitated divorce which well nigh unmans me as I write."

They finally exchange tokens, and part.

Cloten, as I have already explained, represents the bodily personality of Bacon, as being merely the *clothing* of the real man—the phase he was forced by circumstances to wear to his own generation for a covering. *The advances of Cloten to Imogen symbolize the natural desire of Bacon to wed the dramas to his living reputation* and acknowledge them in his own day. The frequent references to *attire* through the play in connection with Cloten determine his symbolical significacy as to its verbalism, while the genius of the character and other points express its intenser application. The following scene of his first introduction has one of these, and also discloses the *bodily* form he symbolizes; and there is some deep pathos of personal satire, considered in its application to Bacon by himself, if carefully digested. It is a conversation between Cloten and two Lords in relation to an encounter of a hostile nature between Posthumus and Cloten:

> "*1st Lord:* Sir, I would advise you to shift a *shirt.* The violence of action hath made you *reek as a sacrifice. Where air comes out air comes in. There's none so wholesome as that you vent."*

The word "shirt" in the above suggests *clothing,* and I have italicised the line satire toward himself of the unappreciated virtuous man whose life was a "sacrifice" to his generation.

"*Cloten*.   If my shirt were bloody, then to shift it."

As though to say, "If my body were stained with dissipation, then, etc."

"*Cloten*.   Have I hurt him?

1*st Lord*.   His body's a passable carcass if he be not hurt.
It's a thoroughfare for steel, if it be not hurt."

Steeled to concealment of feeling, if in good health.

"*2nd Lord*.   His steel was in debt: it went to the back side o the town."

Bacon was once confined for debt, to which this, doubtless, is a satirical allusion.

"*Cloten*.   The villain would not *stand* me."

In the word "stand" there is a direct suggestion as to the incorporeal nature of Posthumus.

"*2nd Lord*.   No, but *he fled forward still, toward your face*."

Bacon's renunciation of poetic fame still looked forward at least to future recognition.

"*1st Lord*.   Stand you! you have *land enough* of your own; but he added to your having: gave you some *ground*."

"Land" and "ground" in the above suggest bodily location, while the satirical idea is that Bacon's consciousness of future fame in the dramas added to his present value with good ground.

"*2nd Lord*.   As many *inches* as you have oceans. Puppies!"

The word *inches* still implies the bodily occupation of room; and the sense is that as many oceans of reserved fame as were in store for Bacon, by so much was he really then a greater man.   The exclamation, "Puppies!" expresses his sense of superiority therefore, to all his contemporaries.

"*Cloten*.   I would they had not come between us."

This means, "I would I need not have been parted from my poetic fame."

"*2nd Lord*.   So would I, till you had measured how *long* a fool you were upon the *ground*."

The words "long" and "ground" here imply, as before, bodily occupancy, having their significance in relation to the symbolical Cloten as the bodily Bacon, but they may also express the author's regret that he should have been forced to separate his name from the plays in the beginning by a rash mistake, *before he had the time to have tested their personal advantage*.

All the foregoing is very pregnant in the allegory.

We have next the beautiful scene of Imogen's questioning Pisanio concerning the departure of Posthumus.

Pisanio is the servant of Posthumus, and *symbolizes the fear of Bacon toward the future perpetuity of the dramas.* Beautiful as this scene is outwardly, it takes on a transformation of divinity, as we read it with its under-meaning in the author's soul as he penned it.

> "*Imogen.* I would thou grew'st unto the shores o' the haven,
> And questioned'st every sail. *If he should write*
> *And I not have it, 'twere a paper lost*
> *As offered mercy his.*"

His in the last line is the folio reading, and I have restored it, as evidently the one designed. It means, that the mercy posthumously offered *the author,* depends upon the preservation of all the plays intact. She continues:

> "*Imogen.*   What was the last
> That he spake to thee?
>
> "*Pisanio.* 'Twas, 'His queen, his queen!' "

Then later, this by Pisanio is filled with the allegorical sense of the fear that clung to Bacon about the perpetuity of the plays, and the last verses express his sad sense of how slowly the barque freighted with his soul must move on to find his recognition compared with the swiftness of his personal career. Their marvellous fitness to both the outward and under meaning exhibits an artistic instance of the singular antithesis of which language is capable:

> "*Pisanio.*   So long
> As he could make me with this eye or ear
> Distinguish him from others. he did keep
> The deck, with glove, or hat or handkerchief,
> Still waving, *as the fits and stirs of his mind*
> *Could but express how slow his soul sailed or,*
> *How swift his ship.*"

In Imogen's reply to this, we learn that the future value of the dramas admonished the author's fears for their preservation to make this value appear " as little as a crow, or less, ere left to after-eye him." that is, that they should be " left " as something of insignificance as much as possible in the eyes of his remaining generation. And his fears reply that they did so. The ingenuity of the allegorical adaptation is superb:

> "*Imogen.* Thou should'st have made him
> *As little as a crow, or less*
> *To after-eye him.*"
>
> "*Pisanio.* Madam, so I did."

It is needless for me to point out here, that it was thus he thought of William Shakespeare, in leaving the plays in his name. But the dramas in their parted fame, would have traced him in their own anxious manifestations, and have proven him by some subtle test, following him until he had melted to the fine air of their own poetry, or had become lost in their tears:

> " *Imogen.*   I would have broke mine eye-strings, cracked them, but
> To look upon him; till the diminution
> Of space had pointed him as sharp as my needle;
> Nay, followed him, till he had melted from
> The smallness of a gnat to air; and then
> Have turned mine eye and wept."

And here we have him at his orisons, as she continues, further on:

> " *Imogen.*   Or I have charged him,
> At the sixth hour of morn. or noon, or midnight,
> To encounter me with orisons, *for then
> I am in heaven for him.*"

That is to say, that through him the heaven of the dramas was at those hours in process of creation.   And she ends:

> " *Imogen.*   Or ere I could
> Give him that parting kiss, which I had set
> Between two charming words. comes in my father,
> And like the tyrannous breathing of the North
> Shakes all our buds from growing."

The succeeding scene, showing the arrival of Posthumus in Italy, may be noted in the allegory chiefly for an allusion to Bacon's brief stay in France in his adolescence.   There is the following conversation respecting Posthumus, by Iachimo, Philario and a Frenchman:

> *Iachimo.*   Believe me, sir, I have seen him in Britain: he was then of a crescent note;* expected to prove so worthy as he hath since been allowed the name of; *but I could then have looked on him without the help of admiration, though the catalogue of his endowments had been tabled by his side, and I do peruse him item by item.*

This last clause is notable for its instant determination of the figure of Iachimo in the allegory.   We know at once of him, what develops more and more in the process of the play.   He *stands for* SLANDER, as is evident by his detraction of Posthumus, and *his absolute symbol in the piece is a slander toward the dramas, endangering their perpetuity.*   The conversation continues:

> *Philario.*   You speak of him when he is less furnished than he is now, with that which makes him, both without and within.

> *Frenchman.*   I have seen him in France; he had very many there could behold the sun with as firm eyes as he.

> *Iachimo.*   This matter of marrying the king's daughter (wherein he must be weighed rather by her value than his own) *words him I doubt not a great deal from the matter.*

That is to say that the fame of the dramas might be detracted from by slanderous rumor.

---

* NOTE.—*Crescendo,* ascending.

"*Frenchman.* And then his banishment.

Iachimo. Ay, and the approbation of those that weep this lamentable divorce under her colours, are wonderfully to extend him; be it but to fortify her judgment, *which else an easy battery might lay flat for taking a beggar without less quality.*"

There is slander, depreciating under cover of praise, while it gloats in the utter defencelessness of its prey. It indicates how easy it was to jeopardize the dramas at their outset, the author being poor and unfriended with the prize of his genius.

It is not necessary to the unveiling of this allegory to recapitulate the portion of its outward form describing the wager upon Imogen between Posthumus and Iachimo.

Omitting it, I will take up next the scene between the Queen and Pisanio, in which she (representing that day and time) says of Imogen (the dramas) as to Cloten's wishes (Bacon's natural desire for the fame of the plays in his life-time):

> "*Queen.* Weeps she still, say'st thou? dost thou think, *in time,*
> *She will not quench;* and *let instruction enter,*
> *Where folly now possesses?* Do thou work;
> When thou shalt bring me word, she loves my son,
> I'll tell thee on the instant, thou art then
> As great as is thy master."

In the portions of the above which I have italicized, there is a converse sense from the one presented, containing a prophecy of the perpetuity of the dramas, and of their being redeemed to become a medium of instruction, instead of being a folly of the stage, corrupt as it then was. The last two lines imply that if Bacon could banish the apprehension of destruction to the future fame of the plays, and were therefore to acknowledge them, it were to overcome his fear.

The Queen proceeds with a brief, but graphic sketch, evidently drawn by Bacon from the reality of his own position as a courtier, at the time this play was written:

> "*Queen.* Greater, for
> His fortunes all lie speechless, and his name
> Is at last gasp. Return he cannot, nor
> Continue where he is: to shift his being
> Is to exchange one day's misery for another:
> And every day that comes, *comes to decay*
> *A day's work in him.* What shall thou expect
> To be a depender on *a thing that leans?*
> *Who cannot be rebuilt, nor has no friends*
> *So much as but to prop him?*"

At the period assigned to the writing of this play, (1609) the biographies of Bacon inform us that he was experiencing the painful sense of long continued repression and repeated disappointments, through the envious machinations of others. The above passage is intensely pathetic, and its sorrow is ennobled by the plaintive regret for delayed opportunities, because "every day that comes, comes to decay a day's work in him."

The beautiful scene of Iachimo's interview with Imogen and the result of the wager, with the Italian's surreptitious entrance into her chamber, and his stealing the bracelet which was the parting token of Posthumus to her, need not here be detailed, although here and there points pertinent to the allegory may be found in it. The author has chiefly used it for the interest of his outward plot, and as a concealment of his allegory, while the incident at the same time lends it a suitable analogy.

The scene of Iachimo's interview with Imogen is followed by another conversation between Cloten and two Lords. It contains a number of ironical hits on the author's personality that involve a study, and ends with the following soliloquy by one of the Lords after the others have made their exit:

"*Lord.* That such a crafty devil as his mother
Should yield the world this ass! a woman, that
Bears all down with her brain; and this, her son,
Cannot take two from twenty for his heart
And leave eighteen. Alas, poor princess,
Thou divine Imogen, what thou endurest!
Betwixt a father by thy step-dame governed;
A mother hourly coining plots; *a wooer*
More hateful than the foul expulsion is
Of thy dear husband, than that horrid act
Of the divorce he'd make! The heavens hold firm
The walls of thy dear honour; *keep unshaked*
That temple thy fair mind; that thou mayst stand
To enjoy thy banished lord, and this great land."

The allusion to the state-craft and intellectual power of England in this passage is marked, as the allegory is understood, as is also that to the writer's separation of his name from the plays for that day, as from an injury, for the sake of their future "honour" to it, and to his "great land." It contains two or three lines which evidently to my mind had a special meaning to the writer, and they have stimulated my curiosity as to what this meaning can have been. They are these:

"—And this, her son,
Cannot take two from twenty for his *heart*
And leave eighteen."

That word "heart" came *from* the heart, I feel. I have surmised the subject in the author's mind may have been his deliberation as to the preserving in the folio, or the discarding from it, of some two of his plays—presuming the passage to have been a final touch at the time of the making-up of the folio. The number of the previously published and unpublished plays in the folio is respectively eighteen. The appearances are that he did come near leaving out even one of these—the *Troilus and Cressida*, but that he "could not find it in his heart " to do so, and hurried it in, at the last, so that it stands un-paged. Again, in another scene, we have Cloten in an ante-room ad-joining Imogen's apartment, conversing with a lord. Under the out-ward bantering there is a touching allusion to Bacon's own " patient " bearing, and exterior calmness under disappointment:

> *1st Lord. Your lordship is the most patient man in loss, the most* coldest that ever turned up ace.

> *Cloten.* It would make any man cold to lose.

> *1st Lord. But not every man patient after the noble temper of your lordship.* You are most hot and furious when you win.

> *Cloten.* Winning would put any man into courage. *If I could get that foolish Imogen I should have gold enough*

After getting a musician to give Imogen a matin song, he knocks at her door, and gives her lady in waiting gold for his admission. But Imogen rebuffs his advances, and breaks out against him thus:

> " *Imogen.*   Profane fellow !
> Wert thou the son of Jupiter, and no more
> But what thou art besides, thou wert too base
> To be his groom: thou wert dignified enough,
> Even to the point of envy, if 'twere made
> Comparative to your virtues to be styled
> *The under-hangman of his kingdom,*
> And hated for being preferred so well."

This great author was so fond of a pun, that in the foregoing he put a very poor one in the line I have italicized. He means by it to express in the allegory that Cloten was the body underhanging the head of which Posthumus was the monarch, as of a kingdom.

Imogen continues:

> " He never can meet more mischance
> Than to be *named* of thee."

Signifying the danger to Bacon's future fame in the plays, if they were connected with his name then. She adds:

> " *Imo.*   His meanest *garment*
> That ever hath but clipped his body, is dearer
> In my respect than all the hairs above thee
> Were they all made such men."

The word "clipped" is pointedly chosen here, as applying to clippings from manuscripts or books, in their relation to posthumous fame. And "garments" in being immediately caught up, and echoed by Cloten repeatedly with much stress, suggests significantly the alle-gorical translation of his name:

> " His *garment?*—nay, the devil · "

And echoed again:

> " His *garment ?* "

And re-echoed:

> " You have abused me—
> His meanest *garment?*

And yet again:

> " I'll be revenged!
> His meanest *garment !* "

In the embassy of Caius Lucius to Cymbeline, with its demand of Roman tribute, there is a designed analogy with the political situation of the day in Britain, which it will be easy for historical students to fit as to the particulars without my help, and it is apart from the main allegory. But there is in the scene a fine passage of national pride as spoken by the Queen, representing the voice of that age, that I will not pass over. It was Bacon himslf, however, as he stood ever in boast and warning the patriot spokesman of his beloved Britain:

> " *Queen.*   Remember, sir, my liege,
> The kings your ancestors : together with
> The natural bravery of your isle, which stands
> At Neptune's park, ribbed and paled in
> With rocks unscaleable, and roaring waters;
> With sands that will not bear your enemy's boats,
> But suck them up to the topmast. A kind of conquest
> Cæsar made here ; but made not here his brag
> Of came, and saw, and overcame ; with shame
> (The first that ever touched him) he was carried
> From off our coast, twice beaten ; and his shipping
> (Poor ignorant baubles!) on our terrible seas
> Like eggshells moved upon their surges, cracked
> As easily 'gainst our rocks : For joy whereof
> The famed Cassibelan, who was once at point
> (O giglot fortune!) to master Cæsar's sword,
> Made Lud's town with rejoicing fires bright,
> And Britains strut with courage."

Cloten remarks:

> " *Cloten.*   Britain is
> A world by itself, and we will nothing pay
> For wearing our own noses:"

And again:

> " *Cloten.* Come, there's no more tribute to be paid. Our kingdom is stronger than it was at that time; and, as I said, there is no more such Cæsars; other of them may have crooked noses, but to owe such straight arms, none: "

And reiterating:

> " *Cloten.* Why, tribute, why should we pay tribute ? If Cæsar can hide the sun from us with a blanket, or put the moon in his pocket,we will pay tribute for light, else, sir, no more tribute pay you now," ·

All these represent Bacon's stand in Parliament on analagous issues of his own day.

Cymbeline says, (speaking as for Britain's fame):

"Son, let your mother end."

That is to say, "Let this age pass, and give way to greater."

As to the point upon which the plot of the drama turns, Iachimo's falsehood respecting Imogen to Posthumus, I need only explain that Iachimo represents a *slander cast upon the dramas* (Imogen), inciting Bacon (Posthumus) through fear (Pisanio) to their destruction   The symbolical character of Pisanio is well sustained.   He is absent from Posthumus, and guarding Imogen, at the time the rash and fatal wager of the former is made.   When Posthumus has heard the slander of Iachimo against Imogen, he is frenzied, and resolves that she must be destroyed.   He therefore writes a letter to her, alluring her to Milford Haven under the pretence that he is there to meet her; and at the same time writes another to Pisanio, telling him of what he has heard to her detriment from Iachimo, and containing the command "Let thy own hand take away her life: I shall give thee opportunities at Milford Haven."   Imogen, on the receipt of her letter is eager to set out, and Pisanio arranges for their instant departure.

When they arrive at Milford Haven, he cannot find it in his heart to obey his master's orders, and kill his mistress, but stands irresolute and hesitating.

His manner and attitude, as thus described in the text, in language put into the mouth of Imogen, would serve an artist, as itself asserts, for a painted representation of the emotion of FEAR; determining his symbol in the under reading:

> "*Imogen.*   Pisanio ! Man !
> Where is Posthumus ?   What is in thy mind
> That makes thee stare thus ?   Wherefore breaks that sigh
> From the inward of thee ?   *One but painted thus*
> *Would be interpreted a thing perplexed*
> *Beyond self-explication.   Put thyself*
> *Into a havior of less* FEAR, ere wildness
> Vanquish my staider senses."

Pisanio, not being able to summon resolution to kill Imogen, then tells her that there is in fact no need for it, since she is already virtually dead by

> "*Pisanio.*   Slander,
> Whose edge is sharper than the sword; whose tongue
> Outvenoms all the worms o' the Nile; whose breath
> Rides on the posting winds, and doth belie
> All corners of the world."

As she, however, entreats to die, since Posthumus has proved recreant to her, yet cannot kill herself, Pisanio still hesitates to do her fateful bidding—telling her it cannot be but that his master has been "abused" respecting her, saying:

> "*Pisanio.*   Some villain, ay, and singular in his art,
> Hath done you both this cursed injury."

He then suggests to her that he might but announce to Posthumus
her death with some "bloody sign" of it, yet leave her still alive.
To that she agrees, asserting that she shall never return to the court
again.

"*Imogen.*   No court, no father, no more ado
With that harsh, noble,* simple nothing
Cloten."

Pisanio rejoins with this advice:

"*Pisanio.*   Now, if you could *wear a mind
Dark as your fortune is;* and *but disguise
That which to appear itself must not yet be
But by self-danger;* you should *tread a course
Pretty and full of view;* yea, haply near
The residence of Posthumus; *so nigh, at least,
That though his actions were not visible, yet
Report should render him hourly to your ear
As truly as he moves.*"

She consents, though it be "peril to her modesty," and he explains to her a project of disguise thus:

"*Pisanio.*   Well, then, here's the point :
You must forget to be a woman, change
Command into obedience ; fear, and niceness,
(The handmaids of all women, or, more truly,
Woman its pretty self) to a waggish courage,
Ready in gibes, quick-answered, saucy, and
As quarrelous as the weasel ; nay, you must
Forget that rarest treasure of your cheek
Exposing it (but O the harder heart,
Alack, no remedy!) to the greedy touch
Of common-kissing Titan, and forget
Your laboursome and dainty trims, wherein
You made great Juno angry."

The foregoing evidently refers to the necessity of giving over the
dramas to the coarse and vulgar stage, as it was in that day, and to the
requirement of their adaptation to it more or less.

Imogen agrees, and Pisanio, having anticipated this result, has
prepared in his *cloak*-bag a youth's disguise, in which he desires her to
attire herself, and offer her services as page to the Roman General,
then on his embassy to the court, and who must pass that way on his
return:

"*Pisanio.*   *Tell him wherein you are happy (which you'll make him know,
If that his head have ear in music).*"

Thus marking her *poetic* symbolism in the allegory.

Pisanio adds:

" *Pisanio.*   Your means abroad
You have me, rich ; and I will never fail
Beginning, nor supplying."

To which she responds:

" *Imogen.*   Thou art all the comfort
The gods will diet me with."

The dramas were, by the allegorical construction of the above, to continue, subsisting in and by *fear*.

From all which foregoing we gather that *a slander had early fallen upon the dramas,* causing the author at first to decide that it were necessary to suppress them, but that *through fear of the great loss to his posthumous fame as a part of British glory, and to all posterity* in so doing, he finally resolved to preserve them under a disguise—even, self-evidently, the disguise of Shakespeare. And, by the way, there is a definite reference in this play, in a previous passage, *to Shakespeare's false title in the dramas,* as well as another allusion to the existing corruptions of the stage. It is put into Iachimo's mouth in his interview with Imogen which I have passed over, to say thus:

" *Iachimo.*   *A lady*
So fair, and fastened to an Empiry
Would make THE GREATEST KING DOUBLE;* to be partnered
With tom-boys, *hired with that self-exhibition*
Which your own coffers yield.' with diseased ventures
That play with all infirmities for gold,
Which rottenness can lend nature; such boiled stuff
As well might poison poison."

In the next scene Imogen is missed from the court. Her father is angered. The Queen rejoices, making this remark, which points definitely her symbolical sense in the allegory:

" *Queen.*   Gone she is
To death or to dishonour: and *my end*
Can make good use of either. She being down
I have the placing of the British crown.'

As much as to say, that with the extinction of the dramas, the one perpetual crown of British poetry would be lost, and only the other comparatively ephemeral productions of the day would remain.

When Cloten learns of Imogen's flight, he resolves to follow her, and be avenged on her for disdaining his suit. He says:

" *Cloten.*   I love and hate her; for she's fair and royal;
And that she hath all courtly parts more exquisite
Than lady, ladies, woman; *from every one*
The best she hath, and *she, of all compounded,*
Outsells them all."

---

* NOTE. "Would make the greatest king double;" there is really no sense in this at all, except in the allegory, when it becomes most luminous.

That well describes *the compound of all female character comprised in the dramas.* He continues:

> "*Cloten.*   I love her, therefore, but
> Disdaining me, and throwing favours on
> The low Posthumus, slanders so her judgment,
> That what's else rare is choked; and in this point
> I will conclude to hate her; nay, indeed,
> To be revenged on her."

At this moment, Pisanio, who has left Imogen at Milford Haven and returned to court, enters, and Cloten furiously demands of him the whereabouts of Imogen. For reply, he presents the letter of Posthumus to Imogen, requesting her to meet him at Milford Haven—supposing her to be by this time departed with the Roman ambassador who has left court, and beyond the reach of pursuit. Cloten then tells Pisanio he has been a good servant to Posthumus, and endeavours to impress him into his own service. Considering Pisanio as Fear, the following is very pointed in its satirical application by Bacon to himself.

> " *Cloten.* Sirrah, If thou would'st not be a villian, but do me true service; *undergo those employments wherein I should have cause to use thee, with a serious industry;* that is, what villiany soe'er I bid thee do, perform it directly and truly. I would think thee an honest man; thou should'st *neither want my means for thy relief,* nor my voice for thy preferment. Wilt thou serve me? for, since patiently and constantly thou hast stuck to the base fortune of that beggar Posthumus, thou canst not, in the course of gratitude, but be a diligent follower of mine. Wilt thou serve me?"

> " *Pisanio.* Sir, I will.

> *Cloten.* Give me thy hand, *here's my purse.*"

This, and the previous clause, "Thou should'st neither want my means for thy relief," intimate very clearly, that Bacon's fears as to acknowledging his dramas often drew upon his "purse" inconveniently. Cloten continues:

> " *Cloten.* Hast any of thy late master's *garments* in thy possession?

> *Pisanio.* I have, my lord, at my lodgings--*the same suit he wore when he took leave of my lady and mistress,*

> *Cloten.* The first service thou dost me fetch that suit thither."
>   [*Exit Pisanio.*]

> " *Cloten.* At Milford Haven.—Even there, thou villain Posthumus, I will kill thee. I would these *garments* were come. She said upon a time that she held the very *garment* of Posthumus in more respect than my noble and *natural person,* together with the adornment of my qualities. *With that suit upon my back I will kill him, and in her eyes.*"

That is to say, he will claim one of the plays to attire his living personality with its fame, and so destroy the possibility of the creation of further dramas for posthumous renown. He proceeds:

"*Cloten.* He on the ground, my speech of insultment ended over his dead body, to the court I'll knock her back, foot her home again."

[*Re-enter Pisanio with the clothes.*]

"*Cloten.* Be those the *garments?*"

"*Pisanio.* Ay, my noble lord.

"*Cloten. Bring this apparel to my chamber; that is the second thing that I have commanded thee; the third is that thou shalt be a voluntary mute to my design.* Be but duteous, and true preferment shall tender itself to thee. My revenge is now at Milford." [*Exit Cloten.*]

That last speech is filled with an inner meaning toward Bacon's fears for his autograph manuscripts of the dramas, and concealment of them.* Pisanio left alone says:

"*Pisanio.* Thou bid'st me to my loss, for true to thee
Were to prove false, which I will never be,
To him that is most true: To Milford go,
And find not her whom thou pursuest."

We are next introduced to the dwellers in a cave of the mountainous region of Wales. They consist of an old man, banished by Cymbeline twenty years previously, and two youths, his adopted sons, but in reality the sons of the king, whom their nurse Euriphile had stolen from their nursery, and delivered to him, for which he had married her, she being since dead. The old man is named BELARIUS, *symbolizing in the allegory the fine air of study and self-discipline* (the name being French Latinized) in which, during the twenty years previously to the writing of this play—that is, from 1589 to 1609—Bacon had mentally retired; showing how early he had entered upon the development of that intellectual and moral self-culture, which was destined to be wrought into a philosophy and a virtuous example for the coming ages.

The two youths were named, respectively, Guiderius and Arviragus, but *the old man had given to each another name, which serves as a confirmatory expletive in the allegory*. He thus describes them. First, Guiderius:

"*Belarius.* This POLYDORE,
The heir of Cymbeline and Britain, whom
The king his father called GUIDERIUS,—Jove!
When on my three-foot stool I sit,† and tell
The warlike feats I have done, his spirits
Fly out into my story: say, thus mine enemy fell,
And thus I set my foot on's neck,—even thus
His princely blood flows in his cheek, he sweats,
And *puts himself in posture
That acts my words.*"

---

* NOTE.—How careful was I when I took my way,
Each trifle under truest bars to thrust;
That to my use it might unused stay
From hands of falsehood, in sure wards of trust.—*Son.* 48.

† NOTE.—*Three-foot stool*, signifying the three kingdoms of study—the physical, the ethical, and the ideal.

The word POLYDORE, lingually interpreted, signifies *Many Ores,** and GUIDERIUS in the same way may be explained to mean, *As a Guide*, while, putting the two together, we arrive at a rendering that implies, *A Philosopher, through many-sided knowledge*. When Belarius relates the feats of discovery, and the triumphs of progress in history, Guiderius puts himself *in posture, that acts*—indicating *the experimental system of Bacon*. Thus, this character represents BACON, THE PHILOSOPHER.

Belarius next describes Arviragus:

> "*Belarius*.   The younger brother, CADWAL,
> Once ARVIRAGUS, *in as like a figure,*
> *Strikes life into my speech*, and *shows much more*
> *His own conceiving.*"

ARVIRAGUS, from the Latin *Ars* (Art) and *Vir* (Man), is translated: *As with the Art of Manhood*.† CADWAL is thus derived: *Cad*, from *Caducarius* (relating to property without a master), and *Val*, from *Validus* (strong, of a healthy complexion); while the two combined may be thus rendered: *Strong and harmonious manhood, through self-government;* and this character symbolizes BACON, THE VIRTUOUS MAN.

The expression, "strikes life into my speech," etc., implies that *the individual, Bacon, moulded study and ethics into original conceptions of his own*.

Elsewhere again, Belarius describes the two in their noble traits possessed in common as reflections of "Nature's" best, by an "invisible instinct":

> "*Belarius*.   O thou goddess,
> *Thou divine Nature, how thyself thou blazonest*
> *In these two princely boys!*   They are as gentle
> As zyphyrs, blowing below the violet,
> Not wagging his sweet head ; and yet as rough,
> Their royal blood enchafed, as the rudest wind
> That by the top doth take the mountain pine,
> And make him stoop to the vale.   'Tis wonderful
> *That an invisible instinct should frame them*
> To royalty unlearned ; honor untaught ;
> Civility not seen from other; valour,
> That wildly grows in them, but yields a crop
> As if it had been sowed."

On our introduction to these mountaineers of the fine air upon the summits of mind, they are emerging from their cave in the early morning. Belarius says to the youths:

---

* NOTE.—In a letter to Sir Henry Wotton, from York House, Oct. 20, 1620, Bacon says : " I shall be very glad to entertain a correspondence with you in both kinds which you write of; for the latter, I am now ready for you, having sent you some *ore* of that mine."

† NOTE.—*Ars* has a meaning as transferred to morals, so far as it is made known by manner of acting, habit, practice, as in the following from *Plautus*: Si inte ægrotant artes antiquæ tuæ; thy former *manner of life*.

> "*Bel.*   A goodly day not to keep house, with such
> Whose roof's as low as ours! Stoop, boys: This gate
> Instructs you how to adore the heavens; and bows you
> To morning's holy office. The gates of monarchs
> Are arched so high, that giants may jet through
> And keep their impious turbans on, without
> Good-morrow to the sun."

And then devotionally:

> "*Bel.*   Hail, thou fair heaven!
> We house in the rock, yet use thee not so hardly
> As prouder livers do."

The youths in turn respond: "All hail!"

Which may be construed that the lowly "roof" of humility teaches adoration and that the gate of knowledge leads to the open "heaven," while study is salutation in its presence.

Belarius continues:

> "*Bel.*   O this life is nobler, than attending for a check;
> Richer, than doing nothing for a bauble;
> Prouder, than rustling in unpaid-for silk;
> Such gain the cap of him that makes them fine,
> Yet keeps his book uncrossed; no life to ours."

Bacon's expression of his own experiences of the two phases.

The youths, however, plead for the privilege of seeing the world, and gaining a knowledge of life, when the old man replies:

> "*Bel.*   Did you but know the city's usuries,
> And feel them knowingly: the art o' the court,
> As hard to leave as keep; whose top to climb
> Is certain falling, or so slippery, that
> The fear's as bad as falling: the toil o' the war
> A pain that only seems to seek out danger
> I' the name of fame and honour, which dies o' the search,
> And hath as oft a slanderous epitaph
> As record of fair act; nay, many times
> Doth ill deserve by doing well; what's worse,
> Must curtsey at the censure. O boys, *this story*
> *The world may read in* ME."

How plainly and sadly does Bacon here depict himself! This passage, or at any rate, the concluding verses, must evidently have been written after his final fall, and in the revision of the play for the folio.

Belarius goes on to describe the cause of his banishment.

> "*Bel.*   My report was once
> First with the best of note. Cymbeline loved me:
> And when a soldier was the theme, my name
> Was not far off: Then was I as a tree
> Whose boughs did bend with fruit: but, *in one night,*
> *A storm, a robbery, call it what you will,*
> *Shook down my mellow hangings, nay, my leaves,*

> *And left me bare to weather.*
> *My fault being nothing* (as I have told you of't,)
> *But that two villains, whose false oath prevailed*
> *Before my perfect honour,* swore to Cymbeline
> I was confederate with the Romans ; so
> Followed my banishment ; and this twenty years
> This rock and these demesnes have been my world ;
> Where I have lived at honest freedom ; paid
> More pious debts to heaven, than in all
> The fore-end of my time."

In the foregoing there is the painful statement of a breach of trust, or "storm," by which Bacon, through "no fault of his own," was, at the outset of his dramatic art, subjected to a virtual "robbery" of his fame in it, and indeed through this, to adequate fame due him otherwise; so that he was forced to pursue his mental avocations in an isolation as lonely and hard as the banishment to a mountain "rock."

Subsequently to the introduction of the mountaineers, there is a scene in which Imogen, having been left by Pisanio, and attired herself in the boy's disguise he had given her, while proceeding on her way to Milford, at first "within a ken," loses herself, and stops, weary and hungry, before their cave. Calling, and receiving no answer, she enters, and seeing food, she begins to eat, when Belarius and his sons returning, look in and behold her with great astonishment, and admiration of her beauty. Belarius says:

> " *Bel.* By Jupiter, an angel! or if not,
> An earthly paragon. Behold divineness
> No elder than a boy."

The beautiful expression is evidently suggested by the Apollo, as figuring the perennial youth of poetry.

Imogen, hearing them, comes out, and apologizes for her intrusion; whereupon the mountaineers question her. She informs them that her name is "Fidèle," and that she is on her way to Milford Haven to meet "a kinsman, bound for Italy." They are all singularly drawn to her, especially the youths, and offer her their hospitality, which she accepts. The next morning the following scene occurs before the cave with the three and Imogen:

> " *Bel.* (*To Imogen.*) You are not well. Remain here in the cave.
> We'll come to you after hunting.
>
> " *Arvir.* (*To Imogen.*) Are we not brothers?
>
> " *Imo.* So man and man should be ;
> But clay and clay differs in dignity,
> Whose dust is both alike. I am very sick.
>
> " *Guid.* Go you to hunting. I'll abide with him.
>
> " *Imo.* So sick I am not : yet I am not well :—
> But not so citizen a wanton, as
> To seem to die, ere sick : So please you, leave me ;

Stick to your journal course : the breach of custom
Is breach of all. I am ill ; but your being by me
Cannot amend me. Society is no comfort
To one not sociable. I'm not very sick,
Since I can reason of it. Pray you, trust me here.
I'll rob none but myself, and let me die
Stealing so poorly.

" *Guid.*   I love thee : I have spoke it,
How much the quantity, the might as much,
As I do love my father.

" *Bel.*   What? how? how?

" *Arvir.*   If it be sin to say so, sir, I yoke me
In my good brother's fault. I know not why
I love this youth, and I have heard you say
Love's reason's without reason. The bier at door,
And a demand who is't shall die, I'd say,
' My father, not this youth.' "

Thus the relationship of the dramas (Imogen) to the philosophy
(Guiderius) and the manhood (Arviragus) of Bacon, asserts itself under
disguise. The last verse implies that Bacon would rather the *Novum
Organum* should die than the dramas; for Belarius is also styled Mor-
gan, to be translated, *My Organ*—meaning the NOVUM ORGANUM of
Bacon.

Imogen turns aside to take a supposed restorative, which Pisanio
had got from the Queen, and given her at parting from her. While
she is doing it, the two youths talk of her, supposing her a boy:

" *Guid.*   I could not stir him ;
He said, he was gentle, but unfortunate ;
Dishonestly afflicted, but yet honest.

" *Arvir.*   Thus did he answer me ; yet said, *hereafter
I might know more.*"

Here is an allusion to a future knowledge of the truth concerning
the plays.

Belarius interrupts the brothers by bidding them join him in the
hunting, and they all tell Imogen to enter the cave and rest, assuring
her they will not be long away, and bidding her hasten and get well,
for she must be their "housewife." She goes within, and the youths
linger to extol the supposed boy to one another:

" *Arvir.*   How angel-like he *sings!*

" *Guid.*   But his neat cookery! He cut our roots in *characters;*
And sauced our broths as Juno had been sick,
And he her dieter.

" *Arvir.*   *Nobly he yokes
A smiling with a sigh*, as if the sigh
Was that it was, for not being such a smile ;
The smile mocking the sigh, that it would fly
From so divine a temple, to commix
With winds that sailors rail at.

> " *Guid.* I do note
> That *grief and patience, rooted to him both,*
> *Mingle their spurs together.*
>
> " *Arvir.* *Grow patience!*
> *And let the stinking elder grief, untwine*
> *His perishing root, with the increasing vine.*"

A dainty first, and then *a divinely pathetic description, in brief, of the spirit of the dramas.* What, but such an under-meaning, could ever have suggested language so exquisite, to depict a fictitious heroine? And it is noticeable that the ostensible incidents could hardly have elicited the delineation.

Cloten, in his pursuit of Imogen and Posthumus, to Milford Haven, arrives now at a forest near the cave of the mountaineers, and soliloquizes:

" *Cloten.* I am near to the place where they should meet, if Pisanio have mapped it truly. *How fit his garments serve me!* Why should his mistress, who was made by him that made the tailor, not be fit, too? the rather (saving reverence of the word) for 'tis said a woman's fitness comes by fits. Therein I must play the workman. I dare speak it to myself (for it is not vain glory for a man and his glass to confer; in his own chamber, I mean) *the lines of my body are as well made as his; no less young, more strong, not beneath him in fortunes, beyond him in the advantage of the time, above him in birth, alike conversant of general services, and more remarkable in single oppositions;* yet this imperversant thing loves him in my despite. What mortality is! Posthumus, *thy head, which is now growing upon thy shoulders, shall within this hour be cut off; thy garments cut to pieces before thy face;* and all this done, spurn thy mistress home to her father; who may, be a little angry for my so rough usage; but my mother, having power of his testiness, shall turn all into my commendations. My horse is tied up safe. Out, sword, and to a sore purpose ! Fortune put them into my hand. This is the very description of their meeting-place."

The actual identity of Cloten and Posthumus, as Bacon and his future fame in the dramas, *is clearly indicated in the lines of the above soliloquy which I have italicized.*

The mountaineers presently meet Cloten, just as he has despaired of finding Posthumus and Imogen. Belarius, who has seen him formerly at the court, recognizes him, and fearful that he has come to seek them as "outlaws," advises that they flee, lest Cloten have an ambush in reserve to take them. Guiderius replies:

> " *Guid.*   He is but one: you and my brother search
> What companies are near: pray you, away;
> Let me alone with him."

It is philosophy solely, that can settle the problem whether or no Bacon's living fame in the dramas must be sacrificed.

The following then occurs between Cloten and Guiderius:

> " *Cloten.*   Soft! what are you
> That fly me thus, some villain mountaineers ?
> I have heard of such.—What slave art thou ?

> "*Guid.*   A thing more slavish did I ne'er, than answering
> A slave without a knock.
>
> "*Cloten.* Thou art a robber,
> A law-breaker, a villain.   Yield thee, thief.
>
> "*Guid.*   To who? to thee?—What art thou?   Have not I
> An arm as big as thine?   A heart as big?
> Thy words, I grant, are bigger, for I wear not
> My dagger in my mouth.   *Say, what art thou?*
> *Why should I yield to thee?*
>
> "*Cloten.* Thou villain base,
> *Know'st me not by my* CLOTHES?
>
> "*Guid.*   No, nor *thy tailor, rascal,*
> *Who is thy grandfather; he made those clothes,*
> *Which, as it seems, make thee.*
>
> "*Cloten.* Thou precious varlet,
> *My tailor made them not.*
>
> "*Guid.*   Hence, then, and thank
> The man that gave them thee.
>
> "*Cloten.* Thou injurious thief,
> *Hear but my name, and tremble.*
>
> "*Guid.*   What's they name?
>
> "*Cloten.* Cloten, thou villain.
>
> "*Guid.*   *Cloten, thou double villain, be thy name,*
> *I cannot tremble at it;* were't toad, or adder, spider,
> 'Twould move me sooner.
>
> "*Cloten.* *To thy farther fear,*
> *Nay, to thy mere confusion, thou shalt know*
> *I'm son to the queen.*
>
> "*Guid.*   I'm sorry for't; not seeming
> So worthy as thy birth.
>
> "*Cloten.* Art not afeard?
>
> "*Guid.*   Those that I reverence, I fear—the wise;
> At fools I laugh, not fear them."

The above is filled with the intense meaning of the allegory. *It is Bacon, the philosopher, parleying contemptuously with Bacon, the personage of his day,* who braves the former, however, to the death; for Guiderius, at length, cuts off his head—that is to say, *Bacon's philosophy overcomes his personal vanity by impelling him to claim nothing of British fame from his own age.*

Guiderius joins Belarius and Arviragus, and informs them what he has done, when they hold a parley over the probability of there being some attendants of Cloten near to arrest them.   The following lines, put in the mouth of Belarius, as spoken of Cloten,

"*Bel.*   Though his humour
                Was nothing but mutation; ay, and that
                From one bad thing to worse,"

speak too sadly Bacon's consciousness of mistake and failure.

Belarius finishes his speech by saying:

"*Bel.*   Then on good ground we fear,
                If we do fear this body hath a tail
                More perilous than the head:"

Intending the probable danger to the future of the dramas by Bacon's personal claim of their authorship, even at his death.

Arviragus replies:

"*Arvir.*   Let ordinance
                Come as the gods foresay it; howsoe'er
                My brother hath done well."

Bacon, in his true manhood, is willing to abide by the chances of time for his just award, but approves, in the light of philosophy, of the present death of his fame.

Then Guiderius says of Cloten:

"*Guid*   I have ta'en
                His head from him; I'll throw it into the creek
                Behind our rock; and let it to the sea,
                And tell the fishes he's the Queen's son, Cloten.
                That's all I reck."

Thus Bacon renounces his fame for that age, and gives it to "the fishes."

And later, Guiderius informs Belarius:

"*Guid.*   I have *sent Cloten's clot-poll down the stream
                In embassy to his mother: his body's hostage
                For his return.*"

Which is a prediction that the contents of Bacon's brain should float down the "stream" of time, a "hostage" for his proper ultimate recognition.

Meantime, during the incident of the encounter and murder of Cloten, Imogen, having taken the specific given her by Pisanio before he left her as a restorative in case of illness, has fallen into a trance from its effects resembling death. This specific Pisanio had received from the Queen, who designed it as a fatal poison, having been deceived in it by her physician and obtained in its place only "a stuff, which being ta'en, would cease the present power of life." Belarius and Guiderius are outside of the cave, when they suddenly hear solemn music. They speak together:

"*Bel.*   *My ingenius instrument!*
                Hark, Polydore, it sounds! But what occasion
                Hath Cadwal now to give it motion? Hark!"

> " *Guid.*   Is he at home ?
>
> " *Bal.*   He went hence even now.
>
> " *Guid.*   What does he mean ? Since death of my dear'st mother,
> It did not speak before. All solemn things
> Should answer solemn accidents. The matter ?
> Triumphs for nothing, and lamenting toys,
> Is jollity for apes, and grief for boys."

Now Belarius, we are told in two places in the drama, was also called MORGAN, which, by a play upon the sound, as I have already explained, is to be translated MY ORGAN, and symbolizes Bacon's great work, the NOVUM ORGANUM.

This is the " ingenius instrument " alluded to by Belarius in the above dialogue, and the reference fixes his symbol in the allegory. Imogen being in a death-trance, as we are presently to see—the dramas being concluded and their true fame dead until futurity, the author has applied himself to that serious work—the first time he has recurred to it since the death of his mother, quite probably, as may be surmised from the allusion. For Arviragus comes out of the cave, bearing Imogen, who is lifeless—the drug of Pisanio having been compounded to create a trance resembling death, instead of as a restorative. Belarius says:

> " *Bel.*   Look, here he comes,
> And brings the dire occasion in his arms
> Of what we blame him for."

The scene that follows is most exquisitely plaintive. It seems the author's prevision of his own obsequies, and a self-pitying tear for the extinction of the divine soul of song that he had revelled in supremely. Arviragus tells the others:

> " *Arvir.*   *The bird is dead*
> *That we have made so much of.*"

Guiderius exclaims:

> " *Guid.*   O sweetest, fairest lily!
> My brother wears thee not one half so well
> As when thou grew'st thyself."

Which means that the beauty of spirit that created the dramas far exceeded the conceptions which they might give of the mind of the man who held their future fame.

Belarius says:

> " *Bel.*   Thou blessed thing!
> Jove knows what *man* thou might'st have made, but I,
> Thou died'st a most rare *boy*, of melancholy!"

Alluding to the early suppression of the author's fame in the dramas, and the " melancholy " interwoven in them, in consequence.

Then comes the description of the way the supposed boy was found dead.

> " *Arvir.*   *Stark, as you see:*
> *Thus smiling, as some fly had tickled slumber.*"

This is followed by the beautiful protestations of Guiderius and Arviragus to make him a worthy grave. Mark how in character each of them speaks:

> " *Guid.*   (*The philosophic Bacon)*
>> Why, *he but sleeps,*
>> If he be gone, *he'll make his grave a bed:*
>> With female fairies will his tomb be haunted,
>> And worms will not come to thee.

> " *Arvir.*   (*The human Bacon)*
>> With fairest flowers,
>> While summer lasts, and *I live here,* Fidele,
>> *I'll* sweeten thy sad grave : Thou shalt not lack
>> The flower that's *like thy face,* pale primrose, nor
>> The azured harebell, *like thy veins:* no, nor
>> The leaf of eglantine, whom, not to slander,
>> *Outsweetened not thy breath:* the ruddock would
>> With charitable bill bring thee all this ;
>> Yea, and furred moss besides when flowers are none
>> To winter round *thy corse.*

> " *Guid.*   (*The philosophic Bacon*)
>> Pry'thee, have done,
>> And *do not play in wench-like words with that*
>> *Which is so serious. Let us bury him,*
>> *And not protract with admiration what*
>> *Is now due debt.*"

And afterwards Arviragus, with his human side, asks, "Where shall we lay him ?" To that, even the philosophic side responds, recognizing the sanctity of the parental bond: " By my good Euriphile, our mother," reminding us of Bacon's wish expressed in his will: " For my burial, I desire it may be in St. Michael's Church, St. Albans, there was my mother buried." Thereafter, the two brothers try to sing a threnody. Arviragus recalls how their mother had been sung to the ground, and would have a repetition of that pious requiem:

> " *Arvir.*   (*The human Bacon)*
>> *Sing him to the ground,*
>> *As once our mother; use like note, and words,*
>> Save that Euriphile must be *Fidele.*"

That " Fidele " is too tender, too tearful, too holy, for comment of mine. It is blotted while I write it with the dew of my sympathy for the divine soul as he penned that record of filial remembrance and fealty unto the union of death.

But Guiderius cannot sing, for, *was it not the music of their tri-partner they were burying?* and *philosophically* he says:

> ' *Guid.*   *I cannot sing: I'll weep, and word it with thee:*
>> For notes of sorrow, out of tune, are worse
>> Than priests and fanes that lie."

Arviragus responds:

"We'll speak it then."

And now Belarius breaks in, and reminds them that they have forgotten to bury Cloten, saying that though he came as an enemy, "he was paid for that," and was yet "a queen's son," and they should "bury him as a prince."

The compensation in store from futurity is the under-meaning of the expression "He was paid for that."

The youths then request him to bring Cloten's body, again speaking respectively in character:

> " *Guid.*   Pray you, fetch him hither.
> *Thersites' body is as good as Ajax.*
> *When neither are alive.*
>
> "*Arvir.*   If you'll go fetch him,
> *We'll say our song* the whilst.   [*Exit Belarius.*]
>
> "*Guid.*   Nay, Cadwal, *we must lay his head to the east ;*
> *My father hath a reason for it.*" ·

The student of Bacon will possibly find this " reason " in the *Novum Organum*.

The brothers sing their dirge, in a song that has been subject to derogatory criticism, and portions of which have been rejected as authentic productions of the same pen as the play. Regarded as Bacon's anticipatory dirge of his own decease, it will be seen how intensely appropriate and pathetic he must have felt it to be, however, and it thus becomes almost impossible to read it without a sympathetic tear. There can be no doubt either of its genuineness, nor of its appositeness of strength and meaning in every line. It will be observed also that Guiderius and Arviragus—the one as the philosopher and the other as the man, in the stanzas and verses respectively assigned to each—preserve their different traits:

SONG.

> " *Guid. (Bacon the philosopher.)*
> *Fear no more the heat o' the sun,*
> *Nor the furious winter's rages ;*
> *Thou thy worldly task hast done,*
> *Home art gone, and ta'en thy wages:*
> Golden lads and girls all must
> As chimney-sweepers, come to dust.
>
> " *Arvir. (Bacon the man.)*
> *Fear no more the frown o' the great,*
> *Thou art past the tyrant's stroke;*
> *Care no more to clothe and eat ;*
> To thee the reed is as the oak ;
> The sceptre, learning, physic must
> All follow this, and come to dust."

Then the brothers alternate a verse in two more stanzas, concluding with a chorus by both. Guiderius says in the former of these:

> " Fear not slander, censure rash ; "

And in the latter:

> " Ghost unlaid forbear thee."

They end the song with the chorus:

> " *Quiet consummation have,*
> *And renowned be thy grave."*

It is peaceful "consummation" that Bacon craves after the fret of his courtier's life, and posthumous renown for his "grave." As to the suggestion of the two foregoing verses quoted, fear of "slander" haunted him all his life, and perhaps the ghost of the unfortunate Essex, whom while he had as a patriot condemned, but still loved, as Brutus Cæsar, was ever "unlaid" in his bosom.

Belarius returns with the body of Cloten, just as they have completed their obsequies, and they lay him down beside Imogen. Belarius says:

> " *Bel.*   Here's a few flowers, but about midnight more ;
> The herbs. that have on them cold dew of the night,
> Are strewings fitt'st for graves.—Upon their faces.—
> You were as flowers, now withered : even so
> These herblets shall, which we upon you strow.—
> Come on, away : apart upon your knees.
> The ground that gave them first has them again :
> Their pleasures here are past, so is their pain."

Thus has Bacon anticipatively performed here the obsequies of his personal fame. I know of nothing so touching in all literature as this imaginative burial, first, of his divine soul of song, as it was known to himself and unknown to others, and as revealed to us in these palpitating dramas; and then of its clothed-on personality, as this was presented to the world, and worn as a necessity of his day, but under inward disclaim and protest. It may be noticed that he has the same burial for both, of herbs and flowers, with no distinction even in the simile. For it was an anticipation, too, of his own death—the death of his spirit of song, and of his bodily part—which, in his self-surrender, would have long to wait for faithful chaplets, saving these woven by himself.

Imogen, being only in a trance, however, awakes as soon as the effects upon her of the drug disappear. She is at first bewildered, and cannot make out where she is. Presently she perceives Cloten's headless body. Then she soliloquizes. Her soliloquy may be read as expressing Bacon's feelings in view of his position, deprived of the true attitude and prestige which should have been his as the known author of the dramas. and of his self-reproaches at the "fear" which he had at first permitted to deprive him of his "head." The double-meaning is intensely "pregnant," and tragic beyond words, though the play is styled a comedy:

> "*Imo* These flowers are like the pleasures of the world:
> This bloody man the care on't. I hope, I dream;
> For so I thought I was a cave-keeper,
> And cook to honest creatures: But 'tis not so;
> 'Twas but a bolt of nothing, shot at nothing,
> Which the brain makes of fumes. Our very eyes
> Are sometimes like our judgments, blind. Good faith,
> *I tremble still with fear.* But if there be
> Yet left in heaven so small a drop of pity
> As a wren's eye, *feared* gods, a part of it!
> The dream's here still, even when I wake,
> It is without me as within me, not imagined, felt.
> A headless man! the garments of Posthumus!
> I know the shape of his leg; this is his hand,
> His foot Mercurial, his Martial thigh,
> The brawns of Hercules; but his Jovial face—
> Murder in Heaven! How?—'tis gone. Pisanio,
> All curses maddened Hecuba gave the Greeks,
> And mine to boot, be darted on thee! Thou,
> Conspired with that irreligious devil, Cloten,
> Hast here cut off my lord.—To write and read
> Be henceforth treacherous! Damned Pisanio
> Hath with his *forged letters*—Damned Pisanio—
> *From this most bravest vessel of the world*
> *Struck the maintop?* O Posthumus! alas,
> Where is thy head? Ah me! where's that?
> Pisanio might have killed thee at the heart
> And left this head on. How should this be? Pisanio?
> 'Tis he and Cloten: malice and lucre in them
> Have laid this woe here. O 'tis pregnant, pregnant!"

There may be read in outburst the whole tragedy of this deprived fame. The foot of Mercury, the thigh of Mars, the muscles of Hercules, the garments even of genius, left a headless trunk, without their proper visage—the "Jovial face" extinct in blank despair, through "fear," and "murder in heaven." Pregnant? Aye, with the death of joy, where joy might worthiest have lived.

The Roman general arrives at Milford Haven, and finds the fleet landed there from Gallia. He comes across Imogen, prostrate upon the dead body of Cloten, and taking her for the page she appears, questions her of the corpse and of herself. She answers him that the body is that of her master, "a very valiant Briton, and a good," and an unequalled master. When the general then inquires his name, she replies:

> "*Imo.* *Richard du Champ. If I do lie, and do*
> *No harm by it, though the gods hear, I hope*
> *They'll pardon it.*"

In the lines I have italicized, there is an allusion to the falsehood of Shakspeare's name in the plays, as being harmless, while the RICHARD *du Champ* contains in itself the intimation of the fatal field whereon the author's dramatic fame was slain betimes.

The Roman offers Imogen service with him, when she says :

> "*Imo.* I'll follow, sir. But first, an't please the gods,
> *I'll hide my master from the flies, as deep*
> *As these poor pickaxes can dig ;* and when
> With wild wood-leaves and weeds I have strew'd his grave,
> *And on it said a century of prayers,*
> *Such as I can, twice o'er,* I'll weep a sigh,
> And leaving so his service, follow you."

Thus we learn why it was that Bacon relinquished his dramatic fame in life and at death. It was in order that he might be "hidden from the flies." But he was also at the same time assured, that this should only be for "a century twice o'er," or thereabouts. How accurately his prophecy hit the length of time it would take for his exhumation! For it was but a little over this predicted two centuries when his name began to be mentioned as the author of the Shakespeare dramas, first in his own country, and then in America.

Next comes a scene in Cymbeline's palace, in which we learn that the Queen is

> "In a fever with the absence of her son,
> A madness, of which her life's in danger :—"

And this, Cymbeline says :

> "*Cym.* In a time
> When fearful wars point at me : her son gone,
> *So needful for the present ;*"

implying Bacon's sense of his usefulness as an adviser to the King.

Cymbeline demands of Pisanio where Imogen is, on pain of torture, who replies that he does not know.

A lord says to the King, speaking of Cloten:

> "*Lord.* Good my liege,
> The day that *she was missing, he was here ;*
> *I dare be bound he's true, and shall perform*
> *All parts of his subjection loyally.*
> For Cloten,
> *There wants no diligence in seeking him,*
> *And will, no doubt, be found.*"

This expresses that although Bacon had bereft England of the true fame of the dramas, he should still ever be found a loyal subject; and for his authorship in the plays, it would come to be diligently "sought," and would, "no doubt, be found "—a prediction which my present rendering of the allegory of this play verifies, in the year 1881, two hundred and fifty-five years after his death.

In the following scene the three mountaineers, hearing the stir of the Roman forces in their neighborhood, consult together what they had better do. Belarius advises that they retire higher in the mountains, as it would be dangerous for them to join the King's party on account of the murder of Cloten. Guiderius tells him this is "a doubt nothing becoming" him, nor "satisfying" them; and Arviragus says it is not likely that they will be taken note of in the excitement of the Roman invasion. Belarius replies:

> "*Bel.*   Besides, *the king*
> *Hath not deserved my service nor your loves ;*
> *Who find in my exile the want of breeding,*
> *The certainty of this hard life ;* aye, hopeless
> To have the courtesy your cradle promised,
> But to be *still hot summer's tanlings, and*
> *The shrinking slaves of winter.*"

That conveys Bacon's sense of wrong in the long want of proper appreciation by King James, and in his insecurity for the prosecution of his philosophical writings.

Guiderius insists on joining the action, since it were "better to cease to be," than to remain in their retreat. And Arviragus says:

> "*Arvir.*   By this sun that shines,
> I'll thither: what thing is it that I never
> Did see man die? scarce ever looked on blood,
> But that of coward hares, hot goats, and venison?
> Never bestrid a horse, save one, that had
> A rider like myself, who ne'er wore rowel
> Nor iron on his heel?   I am ashamed
> To look upon the holy sun, to have
> The benefit of his blessed beams, remaining
> So long a poor unknown."

From which we may conclude that Bacon had, up to the time of writing this play, perhaps up to the time of revising it, three years before his decease, in his studious life, kept aloof from scenes of death and action, and felt it to be censurable.

Belarius, finding that the youths are determined on joining the army, agrees to accompany them.

The fifth act has for its opening scene a field between the British and Roman camps, and Posthumus with the bloody handkerchief sent him in token by Pisanio, in soliloquy of grief:

> "*Post.*   O Pisanio!
> Every good servant does not all commands:
> No bond but to do just ones.—Gods! if you
> Should have ta'en vengeance on my faults, I never
> Had lived to put on this:
> But alack.
> You snatch some hence for little faults; that's love,
> To have them fall no more! You some permit
> To second ill with ills, each elder worse ;

And *make them dread it* to the doer's thrift.
But Imogen is your own : do your best wills,
And make me bless'd to obey!—*I am brought hither
Among the Italian gentry, and to fight
Against my lady's kingdom: 'Tis enough
That, Britain, I have killed thy mistress; peace!
I'll give no wound to thee. Therefore, good heavens,
Hear patiently my purpose: I'll disrobe me
Of these Italian weeds, and suit myself
As does a British peasant: so I'll fight
Against the part I came with; so I'll die
For thee, O Imogen, even for whom my life
Is every breath a death: and thus, unknown,
Pitied nor hated, to the face of peril,
Myself I'll dedicate. Let me make men know
More valour in me than my habits show.*
Gods, put the strength o' the Leonati in me!
*To shame the guise o' the world, I will begin
The fashion, less without, and more within."*

In the foregoing Bacon blames the fear that had at first caused him to disavow the dramas, in doing which he had been permitted "to second ill with ills, each elder worse" in cause of "dread." But he bows to it as destiny—the will of the "gods," to whom the plays belong, and he would be "bless'd to obey."

"I am brought hither among the Italian gentry" has a double sense. *The under-reading is that Bacon has been brought here among the Italian forms of his fiction.* But to be thus known would be "a wound" to Britain; therefore he'll "disrobe of these Italian weeds," and simply be a patriot—so to fight, he says, "*against the part I came with.*". Now there is deep significance in this clause. *The Tempest* is the first play in the folio, placed there, as we now see, according to design—as *Cymbeline* is designedly placed the last—and its characters are *Italian.* Yet this is but one phase of the explanation. *In that play Bacon comes with the enchanter's wand of fiction,* which holds sway over the magic of the whole volume, in resigning the fame of which he disrobes himself of that prestige of his genius, and "fights against the part he came with." The last two verses are a conscious self-deprecation of the fault of outward conformity, which history has ascribed to Bacon. That he himself should thus have deplored it, and recorded his desire to rectify it, redeems it as a serious blot on his name.

A skirmish takes place in the succeeding scene between the Britons and the Romans, wherein Posthumus follows the British army as a poor soldier, and has an encounter alone with Iachimo, in which he vanquishes and disarms him. The battle continues: the British fly, Cymbeline is taken, when Belarius, Guiderius, and Arviragus appear, and shout as follows :

" *Bel.*   Stand, stand ! we have the advantage of ground!
            The lane is guarded : nothing routs us, but
            The villainy of our fears.

" *Guid. and Arvir.* Stand, stand, and fight!"

This is the rallying cry of Bacon to modern philosophy, to take its " stand " on experiment, having " the advantage of ground."

Posthumus appears and seconds the Britons, and Cymbeline is rescued. Then ensues a scene in another part of the field, in which a lord, not knowing that Posthumus had been present, relates to him the desperate situation of the British, when the " strange chance " of " A narrow lane, an old man, and two boys," with the word " Stand, stand," inspired the retreating Britons, and saved the day.

Posthumus replies:

" *Post.*   Nay, you are not to wonder at it : You are made
Rather to wonder at the things you hear
Than to work any. Will you rhyme upon't,
And vent it for a mockery? Here is one :
' Two boys, an old man twice a boy, a lane,
Preserved the Britons, was the Romans' bane.' "

This is, in allegory, the anticipation of the Baconian " lane" or path of induction, and the " stand " is *the pause on a fact for a new rally.* The old man is the *Novum Organum,* and the " old man twice a boy" is the *Cogita and Visa,* which was its first form.

The lord goes, and Posthumus soliloquizes:

" *Post.*   This is a lord! O noble misery!
To be i' the field, and ask, what news of me!
To-day how many would have given their honours
To have saved their carcasses? took heel to do't,
And yet died too. I, in mine own woe charmed,
Could not find death where I did hear him groan;
Nor feel him where he struck. Being an ugly monster,
'Tis strange *he hides him in fresh cups, soft beds,*
Sweet words. Well, I will find him,
For, being now a favourer to the Roman,
No more a Briton, *I have resumed again*
The part I came in: Fight I will no more,
But yield me to the veriest hind, that shall
Once touch my shoulder."

"To be in the field, and ask, what news of me!" means *to exclaim against the folly of the nobility who were living in that day of Bacon himself, and suspended his award to a posthumous age.* The succeeding lines italicized allude by contrast to his willingness to die to personal fame from noble motives: but to his saving a " charmed " immortality, hidden in the " fresh cups, soft beds, and sweet words " of the plays. And to this end, Posthumus adds:

" *Post.*   For me, *my ransom's death;*
On either side I come to spend my breath ;
Which neither here I'll keep, nor bear again,
But end it by some means for Imogen."

This implies, of course, the loss of his personal fame in the plays at his death, for the sake of their preservation to posterity.

Some British captains and soldiers here appear, and arrest Posthumus. At this juncture Cymbeline enters, attended by Belarius, Guiderius, Arviragus and Pisanio. The captains present Posthumus to Cymbeline, who delivers him over to a gaoler.

Next, we have the scene of Posthumus in prison, and soliloquizing as follows:

> "*Post.* Most welcome bondage! for thou art a way,
> I think, to liberty: Yet am I better
> Than one that's sick o' the gout; since he had rather
> Groan so in perpetuity, than be cured
> By the sure physician, *death; who is the key
> To unbar these locks.* My conscience, thou art fettered
> More than my shanks and wrists: You, good gods, give me
> The penitent instrument, to pick that bolt,
> Then, free for ever! Is't enough, I am sorry?
> So children temporal fathers do appease;
> Gods are more full of mercy. Must I repent?
> I cannot do it better than in gyves,
> Desired, more than constrained: to satisfy,
> It of my freedom 'tis the main part, *take
> No stricter render of me than my all.*
> I know you are more clement than vile men,
> Who of their broken debtors take a third.
> A sixth, a tenth, letting them thrive again
> On their abatement: that's not my desire:
> *For Imogen's dear life, take mine: and though
> 'Tis not so dear, yet 'tis a life:* you coined it:
> 'Tween man and man, they weigh not every stamp:
> Though light, take pieces for the figure's sake;
> *You rather mine, being yours.* And so, great powers,
> If you will take this audit, *take this life
> And cancel these cold bonds.* O Imogen!
> I'll speak to thee in silence."

It is plain in the above that, while the author resigns his fame in the dramas to "bondage," he yet blames himself in some sort for the necessity. But we may see in it the struggle it cost him. We can also see in it plainly that his art was the idolatry of his life. How pathetic the lines:

> "For Imogen's dear life, take mine: and though
> 'Tis not so dear, yet 'tis a life:"

And the close, with this its true application, and no fiction, cannot be read without tears for the supreme surrender. Surely, this was the tragedy of tragedies.

But now, as Posthumus sleeps, a vision comes to him. He beholds the apparitions of his father, Sicilius Leonatus, his mother, and two young Leonati, his brothers, who gather around him, and severally address some poetic stanzas to Jove in his behalf, beseeching that "his miseries" be taken off. The Thunderer appears, and rebukes the "ghosts," ordering them back to their "never withering banks of flowers," and telling them it is no care of theirs, but his; adding:

> " *Jove.*   Whom best I love, I cross; *to make my gift*
> *The more delayed, delighted.* Be content,
> *Your low-laid son our godhead will uplift:*
> His comforts thrive, his trials well are spent.
> *Our Jovial star reigned at his birth, and in*
> *Our temple was he married.* Rise and fade!
> *He shall be lord of Lady Imogen,*
> *And happier much by his affliction made.*
> *This tablet lay upon his breast: wherein*
> *Our pleasure his full fortune doth confine,*
> And so away."

He disappears, when the ghosts place the tablet on the breast of the sleeping Posthumus, and vanish. Presently Posthumus awakes, and speaks:

> " *Post.*   And so I am awake.—Poor wretches, that depend
> On greatness' favor, dream as I have done,
> Wake, and find nothing.—But, alas, I swerve;
> Many dream not to find, neither deserve,
> And yet are steeped in favours: so am I,
> That have this golden chance, and know not why.
> What fairies haunt this ground? A BOOK? *O rare one!*
> Be not, as is our fangled world, a garment
> Nobler than that it covers; let thy effects
> So follow, to be most unlike our courtiers,
> As good as promise."

Posthumus then reads from a label this riddle:

> " *When, as a lion's whelp shall, to himself unknown, without seeking find, and be embraced by a piece of tender air; and when from a stately cedar shall be lopped branches. which, being dead many years, shall after revive, be jointed to the old stock, and freshly grow; then shall Posthumus end his miseries, Britain be fortunate, and flourish in peace and plenty.*"

The vision and riddle here given have hitherto, with the short-sightedness of long-time criticism, been regarded as a disfigurement to this play. Indeed, various commentators have styled these "mummery," pronouncing them to be an addition to the piece by another hand and one inferior to that which produced the rest. Some one has supposed that "Shakespeare admitted them because it may have been customary in his day for plays that were put upon the stage to end with a riddle." But it will now be seen that this "riddle" was the gist of the whole volume of dramas ("A book? O rare one!"), committed to posterity confidently; *for evidently the dream has left a BOOK thus labelled for solution.*

Posthumus ends his soliloquy:

> " *Post.*   'Tis still a dream; or else such stuff as madmen
> Tongue, and *brain not:* either both, or nothing:
> Or *a senseless speaking*, or *a speaking such*

As sense cannot untie. But what it is,
The action of my life is like it, which
I'll keep, if but for sympathy."

"Madmen," whose "brains" are incapable of conceiving any special import in this dream and riddle, will simply "tongue" it, nor ever discover its hidden meaning; for it is "a speaking" whose unravelling does not lie within the province of "sense," but belongs to the realm of discernment and apprehension.

A gaoler now enters the prison, and calls Posthumus to come out to his death, be quit of the "contradictions" of earth, and take "the discharge of what's past, is, and to come." The following colloquy ensues:

"*Post* I am merrier to die than thou art to live.

"*Gaol.* Indeed, sir, he that sleeps feels not the toothache. But a man that were to sleep your sleep, and a hangman to help him to bed, *I think he would change places with his officer:* for, look you, sir, you know not which way you shall go.
"*Post. Yes, indeed I do.*

"*Gaol. Your death has eyes in's head then:* I have not seen him so pictured: you must *either be directed by some that take upon them to know,* or take upon yourself that which I am sure you do not know, *or jump the after inquiry on your own peril,* and how you shall speed in your journey's end, I think you'll never return to tell one.

"*Post.* I tell thee, fellow, *there are none want eyes to direct them the way I am going, but such as wink, and will not use them.*

"*Gaol. What an infinite mock is this, that a man should have the best use of eyes, to see the way of blindness. I am sure hanging's the way of winking.*"

Here we have the statement of Bacon's confidence that his fame should rise from its voluntary grave in these dramas. "There are none want eyes," he says, "to direct them the way he is going"—that is, to his ultimate recognition in this play, and in the rest of the dramas —"but such as wink, and will not use them." But I opine, there cannot much longer be such winking; for, "What an infinite mock is this, that men should have the best use of eyes, to see the way of blindness"—imagining that a Shakespeare could have written these mighty dramas.

A messenger enters the prison:

"*Mess.* Knock off his manacles.

"*Post.* Thou bringest good news. I am called to be made free."

This was the previsionary fulfillment to Bacon of his resurrected name in the plays.

The final scene is in Cymbeline's tent. It opens with the entrance of Cymbeline, Belarius, Guiderius, Arviragus, Pisanio, with officers and attendants. Their several symbolisms in the allegory must be kept in mind in their ensuing conversation.

> " *Cym.* (*As Britain's Fame.*)
>
> Stand by my side, you whom the gods have made
> Preservers of my throne. *Wo is my heart,*
> *That the poor soldier that so richly fought,*
> Whose rags shamed gilded arms, whose naked breast
> Stepped before targe of proof, *cannot be found.*
> HE SHALL BE HAPPY THAT CAN FIND HIM,
> IF OUR GRACE CAN MAKE HIM SO."

There is the record of Bacon's promise, in the name of Britain and her "grace," to the one "that can find him" in the dramas.

> " *Bel.* (*As the Fine Air of Thought.*)
>
> I never saw
> Such noble fury in so poor a thing ;
> Such precious deeds in one that promised nought
> But beggary and poor looks."

That alludes to the little advantage Bacon reaped in his life-time from his superiority.

> " *Cym.* No tidings of him ?
>
> " *Pisanio.* (Fear.)
> *He hath been searched among the dead and living,*
> *But no trace of him.*
>
> " *Cym.* (*To Belarius, Guiderius, and Arviragus, as the works, philosophy and character of Bacon.*)
> To my grief
> *I am the heir of his reward, which I will add*
> *To you, the liver, heart and brain of Britain,*
> *By whom, I grant, she lives.*"

The Roman general, Imogen, Posthumus, Iachimo, and the rest of the Roman prisoners, are now brought into the King's presence, when a general *denouement* takes place. Cymbeline discovers Imogen to be his daughter, recognizes Posthumus in the soldier who had saved the battle to him, and restores them to each other, in honor and happiness, Iachimo confessing his villainy. Cymbeline says here, in his astonishment at these revelations:

> " *Cym.* Does the world go round ?
> *If this be so, the gods do mean to strike me*
> *To death with mortal joy.*"

So should British fame at this restoration to her immortal Bacon of his poetic laurels be stricken " with mortal joy "

When Cymbeline's daughter then speaks, he exclaims, spellbound:

> " *Cym.* The TUNE of Imogen !"

As much as to say, " The POETRY of Bacon's imagination !"

The King proceeds to tell Imogen that her mother is dead, and when she expresses her regret, he responds:

> "*Cym.*   Oh, she was nought, and 'long of her it was
> That we meet here so strangely."

It was on account of the emptiness of Bacon's age, that the true fame of the dramas, in his name, must meet them so late.

Belarius next becomes known to the king, as "old Morgan," whom he had "sometime banished," and presents to him Guiderius and Arviragus, as his own long-lost sons, and brothers to Imogen. Then Cymbeline says:

> "*Cym.*   Oh, what, am I
> A MOTHER to the birth of THREE? Ne'er MOTHER
> Rejoiced deliverance more. *Bless'd may you be*
> *That after this strange starting from your orbs*
> *You may reign in them now.*"

That "mother," twice over, should long ago, except for criticism's "seeing the way of blindness," have suggested the allegorical sense of *Cymbeline*. By "three" is designed the three orders of fame due to Bacon, as philosopher, man and poet—these having been strangely "started from their orbs," but henceforward "to reign in them."

Cymbeline, however, fears that by the restoration to Imogen of her brothers, she has "lost a kingdom," when she replies:

> "*Imo.*   No, my lord,
> *I have got two worlds by't.   O my gentle brothers,*
> *Have we thus met?* O never say hereafter,
> But I am truest speaker: you called me brother
> When I was but your sister.   I you brothers
> When you were so indeed."

Cymbeline delights in the "instinct" which drew the brothers and sister thus at once together, but wishes for further developments hereafter at fitting "time" and "place : "

> "*Cym.*   When shall I hear *all through? This fierce abridgement*
> *Hath to it circumstantial branches, which*
> *Distinction should be rich in.* Where? how lived you?
> And when came you to our Roman captive?
> How parted with your brothers? how first met them?
> Why fled you from the court? and whither?
> These, and your THREE MOTIVES *to the battle,* with
> I know not how much more, should be demanded,
> And all the other by-dependencies
> From chance to chance : but nor the time nor place
> Will serve our long interrogatories."

This is Bacon's demand for similar investigation of the foregoing dramas (the play of *Cymbeline* being the last in the folio of 1623), for the filling out of the "fierce (proud) abridgement" of his discovery in this play, in "circumstantial" revelations which "distinction should be rich in," in the other dramas, as to his concealed authorship—its cause, origin, the "three motives" for its maintenance throughout all his life, and at his death.

Cymbeline continues:

"*Cym.* See,
Posthumus anchors upon Imogen,
And she, like harmless lightning, throws her arms
On him, her brothers, me, her master, hitting
Each object with a joy: the counterchange
Is severally in all. Let's quit this ground,
And smoke the temple with our sacrifices.—"

The above is Bacon's prediction, that this restoration of the dramas, in tri-partnership with his philosophy, and his virtuous character, known at last in its true light, to Britain's fame, should fall suddenly, "like harmless lightning," with "counterchange" of "joy."

Cymbeline adds to Belarius:

"*Cym.* Thou art my brother: so we'll hold thee ever."

The *Novum Organum* is here declared "brother" to Britain's fame by its omnipotent and omniscient author—a declaration which Britain would do well to bear in mind.

The play closes with the narration by Posthumus of the dream he had while in prison, and his handing the "label" left on his bosom to a soothsayer to expound. The soothsayer, after reading the riddle aloud, explains it thus:

"*Sooth.* Thou, Leonatus, art the lion's whelp,
The fit and apt construction of thy name,
Being Leo-natus, doth import so much."

To Cymbeline:

"*The piece of tender air, thy virtuous daughter.*"

(An ambiguity characteristic of the soothsayer's art follows here, and the explanation continues:)

"*The lofty cedar, royal Cymbeline,*
Personates thee: and thy lopped branches point
Thy two sons forth: who, by Belarius stolen,
For many years thought dead, are now revived,
To the majestic cedar joined: whose issue
Promises Britain peace and plenty."

With the foregoing hints, I find no difficulty in giving the subjoined absolute

SOLUTION OF THE RIDDLE.

When, at the time that a posthumous fame born of a (British) lion, shall, unconsciously and without seeking, find itself embraced by the tender "Ariel" of its own BOOK, O RARE ONE! and when the branches

of Bacon's Poetry, Philosophy and Virtue, which, lopped from the stately cedar of Britain's renown, have been dead many years, shall afterwards revive, be jointed to the old stock, and freshly grow, then shall the misery of his delayed recognition terminate, Britain be fortunate, and flourish in peace and plenty.

Here is a correspondence with the passage of Bacon's Will, which reads: " For my name, I leave it to other nations, and *the next ages.*"

The unfolding of this enigma, shows us that he knew confidently, that his name would be restored to all the honor to which it is entitled, and engrafted on the spreading cedar of British renown, there freshly to grow to her immortal fame. This play was his prophecy thereof— prophecy to him being " itself a species of history, with the preroga- tive of deity stamped upon it, of making all times of one duration, so that the narrative may anticipate the fact." Thus also, he says, "The mode of promulgating ratiocination by vision, or the heavenly doctrines by *parable, partakes of the nature of poetry.*" It is seen here, how he has woven this prophecy concerning himself in poetical allegory.

For myself, nothing has convinced me more of the power of this great man, than the prescience exhibited in this assurance of the world's future recognition of him in these dramas, and of his ultimate restor- ation to the full tribute due to his trifold name, as Philosopher, Man, and Poet.

People of Great Britain, and Members of the New Shakspere So- ciety, of London, in reference to the revelation I have here made known, I would call your attention particularly to its evolutionary process, from its incipiency unto this its ultimate unfolding, as being perfectly in accordance with the law of all discovery. About twenty-five years ago —by one of those strange coincidences which interweave an element of the miraculous in the adaptations of human events—a lady of this country, named Delia *Bacon,* first detected a mysticism in these dramas, suggesting to her another meaning underlying the apparent one, and convincing her of Lord Verulam's hand in their creation. To set forth her views, she published a book, which fell still-born from the press, and died herself soon after of the disappointment. I have never seen her work, but I have understood she claimed in it, that the so- called Shakespeare dramas contain a "cipher" which, being read, would show that they were written for the purpose of elucidating the Baconian philosophy. Hence the title of her book: "*The Philosophy of Shake- speare's Plays Unfolded*" The accounts of her state, that she also be- lieved there could be found in Shakespeare's grave a key to the "cipher" she supposed she had detected in the plays—the anathema on the dis- turbers of which, she conceived designed for the preservation of this "key," until such time as the discovery of the "cipher" should de- mand it. Here, you perceive, was a broach upon the truth, accom- panied with error, as the first advancements toward discovery always necessarily are.

Subsequently to this primary breaking of the ground, there has been a growing tendency among critics of these plays, to the notion of some concealed significance, in passages of them, at least. And about three months since, I was surprised to receive a letter from a gentleman concerning the probable Baconian authorship, pointing out to me the derivative symbolism of names in some of the dramas—supposing, as I had, that no one had detected this but myself—although, I should add, that none of his explanations accorded at all with my own.

All this is only evidence that the time has been ripening toward that recognition and revelation of the enigma of these dramas to which I here invite you. It is the greatest of mankind appealing to you from the tomb of his magic volume, in the miracle of his own prophecy, to inscribe it henceforth with his resurrected name.

I am aware that the kind of proof you must accept in this case is of a singular nature—so singular, indeed, that it can only address itself to the highest order of minds. What you are expected to recognize here is, in fact, as far above the average capacity as are the equations of the differential calculus. But to the discerners, the respective truths can be no less positive in the one instance than in the other. This is truth pressed home by analogy—the sphere neither of logic nor of mathematics, but the sphere equally of certainty to those minds which can grasp it. The proof here is of that order by which we are compelled at last to accept all the highest truths we have. It is that kind of truth which is involved in no formula, but compels recognition upon abstract grounds. Still, there are vital objective points to negative the refusal of it. Coincidences, as I have just said, are marvellous. But there are some things that can never have been fitted together by coincidence: such as the adjustment of the names of the *dramatis persona* to their appropriate symbols as I have here presented them to you, and these to the genius of their several personifications in the situations and development of this play. If you explain the allegory of Bunyan by the names of the characters and the fitness of these to the names, you cannot evade the similar explanation of *Cymbeline*. It could have been no coincidence on the part of the writer, that sixteen names given to personages are adapted to a symbolism working out a consistent and harmonious result, sustaining a perception that has otherwise partially obtained among the students of these plays, that they are the production of Francis Bacon. Neither could any accident or ingenuity on my part have effected this dove-tailed construction of the piece. It is noticeable also that there are certain expressions in the play which have no possible meaning except in the light of this discovery—such as these:

> " A lady
> So fair, and fastened to an empiry,
> Would make the greatest king double."
>
> " My ingenious instrument."
>
> " A mother to the birth of three."
>
> "Three motives to the battle."

The rendering of the closing enigma without a flaw, cannot either, have been the result of any adroitness of mine. In short, nothing else than an absolute reading of the mind of the writer, in the allegorical construction of *Cymbeline*, could ever have produced this harmonious and miraculous revelation, as it is now laid before you. To myself, my rendering of this play comes as the seal and proof of an allegorical sense that I had two years and a half since detected in the sonnets by the same hand, and subsequently discovered to be pursued in the volume of dramas—the sonnets proving, in fact, a key to the under-reading of the plays. I feel that my penetration into, and unfolding of the inmost mind and heart of these plays, is a realization of the deepest reach of sympathetic intuition of which the human intellect and soul are capable—only short of that attained by the immortal dramatist himself, who now posthumously claims his "BOOK, *O, rare one!*' at your hands.

It is for you whom I address, by accepting his appeal of prophetic history, to dethrone an impracticable myth, and immediately re-engraft with all fitting *eclat* in the spreading cedar of your native Britain, the tri-fold fame of

> "Large browed Verulam,
> The first of those who know."

Will you not bid me say, in joy of my achievement, "Come forth, now, god of my soul, called by your own pre-ordered miracle to be found of your kindred mate, cast off the mask of two centuries and a half, receive with that of your "Imogen," *my* "tender-air embrace," and take from my vibrating hands your posthumous fame, to resound the British Cymbal."

Thus, members of the New Shakspere Society, and people to whom the true fame of England is dear in her illustrious names, you have my disclosure, and its inclusive and inevitable appeal. I would respectfully suggest that you take action immediately upon these as to the expediency of your receiving my exposition of the other dramas. I may remark that such exposition includes a disclosure of the author's primary reasons for giving over the reputation of the plays to Shakespeare, and reveals an absolute divineness of ideality in them, never hitherto conceived, in all the laudative dissection and criticism which have been lavished on them. As there was a reason for the placing of *Cymbeline* at the end of the folio, so there was, similarly, one for the putting of the *Tempest* at the beginning, as I am prepared to show you. And I can unfold to you the same allegorical, or semi-allegorical, under-reading more or less carried on throughout the plays, forming an explanation of words and passages hitherto admitted to be hopelessly obscure. As I have already said in my prefatory remarks, my health is precarious, so that I am liable to be called from the world at any time, leaving this important discovery but thus partially revealed. Therefore, if your action shall approve the reception and formal announcement of my revelation, I request that your Society communicate with me as to placing my discovery in a shape that shall best redound to Lord Verulam's restituted name in these dramas before the literary world.

Whatever your decision may be, however, I am assured that the recognition of Bacon's title cannot much longer be delayed. Truth and justice must, in the course of human events, assert their own vindication. Thus, as confidently as Bacon committed to the play of *Cymbeline* his prophecy of the final discovery of his proper fame, even so confidently do I here place on record my prediction that, twenty-five years hence, the rendering I have given of it will prevail, and that he will be accepted as the real author of the works so long falsely attributed to Shakespeare.

I have the honor to be, yours, with great respect,

CATHARINE F. ASHMEAD WINDLE,

(Of Philadelphia).

———

Address: Mrs. C. F. ASHMEAD WINDLE,

107 FIFTH STREET,

SAN FRANCISCO, CALIFORNIA,

United States of America.

www.ingramcontent.com/pod-product-compliance
Lightning Source LLC
Chambersburg PA
CBHW030906050726
47500CB00009B/1131